KENNETH GRAHAME'S
THE WIND IN THE WILLOWS
IN EASY READING VERSE

By the same author:

Shakespeare's Tragedies in Easy Reading Verse

Shakespeare's Comedies in Easy Reading Verse

Shakespeare's Histories & Romances in Easy Reading Verse

Shakespeare's Sonnets in Easy Reading Verse

Chaucer's Canterbury Tales in Easy Reading Verse

Charles Dickens' A Christmas Carol in Easy Reading Verse

Charles Dickens' Oliver Twist in Easy Reading Verse

KENNETH GRAHAME'S
THE WIND IN THE WILLOWS
in Easy Reading Verse

Richard Cuddington

Cover design by Denis Grigorjuk
Illustrations by Michael Avery

Published by CompletelyNovel.com

ISBN 9781849149563

Contents

The River Bank   2

The Open Road   14

The Wild Wood   30

Mr Badger   48

Mr Toad   66

Toad's Adventures   92

The Further Adventures of Toad   118

Summer Tears   148

Toad's Homecoming   178

'How are you Mole?' enquired the Rat

THE RIVER BANK

Mole was working very hard
With duster, pail and mop,
When a tired back and aching arms
Encouraged him to stop.

'Blow and bother, drat it all!
I've had enough of this.
If I spring clean the whole day long
I don't know what I'll miss.'

So he scraped and scratched and scrabbled
And scrooged, then scrooged some more,
Calling, 'Up, up, up we go!'
Till his little paws were sore.

But then at last his velvet snout
Pushed through the soft, dark ground;
And trembling with excitement
He took a look around.

He ran across the meadow
Among the budding flowers,
And thought there was no finer way
To spend the passing hours.

He thought his joy was quite complete
But then the Mole espied
A full fed river flowing,
Very deep and very wide.

It was the first time Mole had seen
A gushing, running river;
It gurgled and it chuckled
And put him in a quiver.

It shook and brightly shimmered,
It clattered and lightly danced,
It made the Mole feel happy,
Joyful, spellbound and entranced.

He listened to the water
Babbling on its way,
And then he sank down on the grass –
Oh, what a splendid day!

But as he sat upon the bank
And looked across the river,
He saw within a deep, dark hole
A sight that made him shiver.

Something very bright and small
Twinkled in the hole;
It vanished – then it reappeared;
It slightly chilled his soul.

Could it be a twinkling star?
That would be out of place,
And a glow-worm quite that large
Just couldn't be the case.

Then as he looked it winked at him
From deep within the hole;
And then a face began to grow,
Which startled timid Mole.

Small neat ears and silky hair,
Just like a Persian mat…
'Well, goodness me!' exclaimed the Mole,
'Why, it's the Water Rat.'

'How are you Mole?' enquired the Rat.
'Quite well,' replied the Mole.
'You really took me by surprise
Emerging from your hole.'

The Rat did not respond at first
But presently enquired,
'Would you like to join me here
If you're not feeling tired?'

'An easy thing for you to say,'
Mole pettishly replied,
'But how do you suggest that I
Get over to your side?

'I cannot swim a stroke you know.
Why I can't even float.'
So Rat hauled on a line and then
Revealed a sleek, blue boat.

He rowed across the river
And said, 'Step lively now.'
So Mole took an almighty leap
And landed in the bow.

'Oh my, oh my!' the Mole exclaimed
Collapsing in a seat,
'This really is tremendous fun.
An unexpected treat.'

'The river's great,' the Rat replied.
'No better place than this.
The finest in the whole wide world,
It is, it simply is.'

They rowed beneath the shady trees
And Rat began to muse
About the joys of taking
A small boat for a cruise.

'Whether you get far away
Or if you drift and float,
It really doesn't matter;
Time's not wasted in a boat.'

Then he looked at Mole and said,
'It's turned to such fine weather,
Shall we pack a picnic lunch
And row downstream together?'

Mole wiggled all his toes with glee
And sighed with deep content,
'Oh what a day I'm having –
The best I've ever spent.'

'Wait a minute then,' said Rat,
'For I've a little hunch
That we might get quite hungry,
So let me pack some lunch.'

Returning with a hamper,
'Here's our lunch,' Rat cried.
Mole looking at the basket, thought,
'I wonder what's inside.'

They hardly spoke a single word
As they went on their way,
For both of them were savouring
Each moment of the day.

Presently they moored the boat –
Laid food out on some rugs.
They had sliced ham and bread and cheese
And tea in yellow mugs.

'The finest meal I've ever had!'
Mole finally declared.
'Yes, really quite the very best
In which I've ever shared.'

He lay back, replete and happy,
His mind quite free of troubles,
When through his sleepy, half-closed eyes
He saw a streak of bubbles.

'Bubbles! Oho!' exclaimed the Rat
In a cheery sort of way.
'If it's not my friend the Otter –
Well, this really makes my day.'

'Greedy beggars,' Otter said,
Shaking water from his coat.
'Is the food all gone - perhaps
There's some left in the boat?'

Rat ignored his question,
Saying, 'Otter, meet the Mole.'
'Pleased to meet you,' Otter said,
Gazing at an empty bowl.

Then they heard a rustling noise
Within a nearby hedge;
They saw a large and stripy head
Peer at them round the edge.

'It's Badger,' shouted happy Rat,
'So how are you today?'
'Hmm… company,' Badger grunted,
And hurried on his way.

The Rat looked disappointed.
Mole said, 'What's that all for?'
The Rat replied, 'It's just his way –
Thinks everyone's a bore.

'Now Otter – who is out today
Enjoying all this sun?'
Otter pulled a face at Rat;
'Well, Toad is out for one.

'He's in his brand new rowing boat,
For that's his latest fling,
All dressed up to look the part –
New togs, new everything.'

Then suddenly they caught a glimpse
Of a new boat gushing past;
The rower – clearly hard at work
Still wasn't moving fast.

He was short and very fat
And sweating as he rowed;
'Well I'll be…' the Rat exclaimed,
'Look over there, it's Toad!'

Rat called across but red-faced Toad
Just settled to his work.
Rat said, 'I've never known old Toad
Avoid a chance to shirk.'

Then an errant mayfly swerved
And disappeared from view;
And plop! – a splash of water,
And Otter was gone too.

'Well,' said Rat, 'I think it's time
We started heading back.'
He turned and asked the willing Mole
To clear the bowls and pack.

Mole gathered all the dirty bowls
And remnants of the food,
And then they rowed towards Rat's home,
Both in a dreamy mood.

The Rat recited poetry
As they went on their way;
They watched the fiery, setting sun
Bring on the close of day.

'May I row?' the Mole enquired.
'Please let me have a go.'
'No, no, my friend,' the Rat replied.
'You have to learn to row.'

Mole fell to thinking quietly,
Then thought and thought some more;
And then he pushed the Rat aside
And grabbed the nearest oar.

'Stop it, Mole!' the Rat cried out,
But Mole paid him no heed;
He dug the oar in deeply and
Brought up a clump of weed.

Next time he missed the surface,
His legs flew o'er his head –
Then sploosh and over went the boat:
Mole sank to the riverbed.

He spluttered and he coughed and wheezed
Until his throat was sore;
Then something grabbed him by the neck:
It was Rat's furry paw.

He could feel the Rat was laughing,
He could feel it through Rat's arm;
It quelled Mole's fear of drowning
And calmed his deep alarm.

Rat pulled the Mole onto the bank;
He said, 'Now you see why
I was so hesitant to let
You go and have a try.'

Rat recovered all his things
And dragged them to the shore.
Mole begged the Rat to let things be
The way they'd been before.

'Rat, my good and generous friend,
Forgive my foolish prank;
You shouldn't let me closer to
The river than the bank.'

'That's all right,' the Rat replied,
'Forget it, let things be.
Think no more about it –
Now let's go home for tea;

'And why not come and stay with me
In my home awhile;
Although it's very plain you'll see
It has a certain style.'

The Mole was clearly deeply touched
And brushed away a tear;
The Rat ignored his muffled sobs
Pretending not to hear.

Finally they reached Rat's home
And moored the boat with care;
Rat built a roaring fire and then
Gave Mole his finest chair.

He told him tales till supper time
Of herons, weirs and pike;
Of Otter, Toad and Badger too –
What he was really like.

Then later on that evening
When both were amply fed,
They said, 'Goodnight, God bless, sleep well,'
Then tottered off to bed.

Mole curled up beneath his sheets
And gave a happy sigh;
He drifted off to sleep and with
The river gurgling by.

'Come inside and look around,
I planned it all – I did!'

THE OPEN ROAD

The summer days passed gently by,
Each one a joy to savour,
Until one day Mole turned to Rat
To ask a simple favour.

'Ratty, I was wondering
Could we please make a call,
Upon your good friend, Mr. Toad,
At his grand home, Toad Hall?'

'Why yes, of course,' replied the Rat,
Then jumping to his feet,
He added, 'Toad is always keen
To show his country seat.

'He'll be so pleased to see us
And it's a pleasant row;
He always seems downhearted
When it comes time to go.

'Perhaps he's not too clever;
Too proud for his own good,
But this of course he won't admit –
He feels misunderstood.'

Mole rowed along the river
Until they reached Toad Hall;
An ancient house of mellow brick,
Imposing, wide and tall.

Well-kept lawns sloped gently down
Right to the water's edge,
And all the grounds were bordered by
A high green privet hedge.

'Moor up in the boathouse Mole,
It should be safe in there.'
Mole did as Rat requested and
Made sure to take great care.

Mole stood gazing at the boats
All slung across the beams.
'He's tired of boats,' the Rat remarked.
'They're Toad's forgotten dreams.'

They set off then across the lawn
Which had been freshly mowed,
Then turning round a corner
They came upon the Toad.

A map was open on his lap;
He laughed and cried 'Hooray!
This is splendid Rat, my friend –
You've really made my day.

'I'm very glad you both have come.
What luck you should appear!
I'd just this minute sent a note
Insisting you come here.'

'What a lovely house!' said Mole,
As Rat sat in a chair.
'Finest on the bank,' said Toad –
'Fact – finest anywhere.'

Rat gave Mole a knowing wink
And slightly ducked his head,
But Toad saw what the Rat had done –
His face turned very red.

For a moment silence reigned.
(Mole thought they'd have to go)
Then Toad let out a merry laugh –
'It's just my way you know.

'And dear Rat, you must admit
That it's not bad at all;
In fact I know you're very fond
Of my dear home, Toad Hall.

'So let's be sensible, my friends –
I need your help you see.'
'If it's with rowing,' Rat replied,
'You'll get no help from me.'

'Oh pooh to boating,' cried the Toad,
'A silly, boyish prank;
Up and down the river and
The same old river bank.

'It makes me downright sorry
To see you waste your time,
You ought to know much better, Rat,
It really is a crime.

'No, I have found the real thing –
I rue the wasted year –
Come with me, the pair of you,
Come quickly – over here.'

He led them to the stable yard,
So excited that he ran,
And there they saw to their surprise
A gypsy caravan.

Bright canary yellow,
The wheels were red and green.
'I'll bet you anything,' cried Toad,
'It's the nicest one you've seen.

'You must admit there's so much fun
Contained within that cart,
For those with an enquiring mind
And wandering in their heart.

'The open road, the rolling downs,
A life devoid of sorrow;
Here today then up and off
To somewhere else tomorrow.

'Come inside and look around,
I planned it all – I did!'
With trepidation in their hearts
They did as they were bid.

It was compact and homely –
Toad hadn't been a liar –
The caravan had everything
An animal could desire.

'It's all complete, you see,' said Toad,
'To make a start quite soon;
In fact I thought we might set off
Some time this afternoon.'

'I beg your pardon,' said the Rat,
'You assume too much, you know.
What makes you think we've got the time,
Or even want to go?'

'Now, dear Ratty,' Toad replied,
'Don't take that sniffy way;
I can't do this without you and
We must set out today.

'It's settled so don't argue –
It's something I can't stand;
You know you like to be around
To lend a helping hand.

'You can't stay by that river
With so much else to see,
And you will see it all and more
If you both come with me.'

'I'll say it once and that is all,
I'm not coming, Toad,' said Rat.
'I'm staying by the riverside,
And I insist – that's that!'

They argued back and forth until
At last Toad won the day;
It wasn't so surprising as
He always got his way.

And so it was that after lunch –
And after some more talk –
They set off with the horse and cart,
Delighting in their walk.

Very late that evening
And many miles from home,
They camped upon some common land
And freed the horse to roam.

They ate a simple supper
On the grass beside the cart,
Then climbed into their cosy bunks –
They'd need an early start.

'Goodnight, you two,' said happy Toad.
'I'm sure you're having fun.
The really splendid thing is that
Our trip has just begun.

'Talk about your river, Rat,
You can't beat the open road.'
'I never mention it,' said Rat.
'I know you don't,' said Toad.

'It's in my mind though all the time,'
Said Rat in muffled tone.
'We could go home,' Mole whispered,
'And leave Toad on his own.'

'No, we'll see it out,' said Rat.
'It shouldn't take too long.'
When it came to Toad's behaviour
The Rat was seldom wrong.

~ ~ ~

Next day old Toad lay fast asleep
And showed no sign of waking;
He did not even grunt or stir
At Mole's continual shaking.

So Mole and Rat got cracking
With all those little chores
That are so much a part of life
When in the great outdoors.

At last they set off on their way
Along a dusty lane.
Toad talked on incessantly –
Of course his talk was vain.

Rat was saying now and then,
'Yes, yes I know it's so.'
But his curt manner made it clear
He didn't want to know.

Mole was walking with the horse
To keep him company,
For he'd complained to each of them:
'No-one speaks to me.'

So Mole had had a little chat;
The horse was quick to say
It made a difference to him as
They went along their way.

Then from behind they faintly heard
A hum just like a bee;
Looking back a cloud of dust
Was all that they could see.

Approaching at enormous speed,
'Poop, poop' and 'poop' again,
It roared out like an animal
In a hopeless state of pain.

The peaceful scene was shattered
By a blast of wind and sound;
'Poop, poop' – and it was on them
Before they could turn around.

It was a huge, red motor car,
A beast made all of steel
With its driver tense and manic
Hunched over at the wheel.

They jumped into the nearest ditch
Deafened by the roar;
And then it dwindled to a speck –
Became a bee once more.

The horse who had been dreaming, reared –
Mole held him by the neck.
The cart rolled over in a ditch
And lay a hopeless wreck.

'Villains – scoundrels!' shouted Rat.
'I'll get the law on you.
I'll drag you all through every court
Before I'm good and through.'

'Poop, poop' and 'poop' again – the words
Came quietly from Toad.
He sat with legs and arms outstretched –
Spread-eagled on the road.

Mole and Rat were trying hard
To right the damaged cart.
They hoped that they could sort the mess
And make another start.

Alas, the caravan was smashed
And seemed beyond repair.
'Toad should be very cross,' said Mole,
'But doesn't seem to care.'

'Toad,' cried Rat, 'Get over here
And lend a helping hand.'
But Toad said not a single word –
Made no attempt to stand.

He sat there in a sort of trance,
A smile upon his face.
'Come on, Toad,' the Rat cried out.
'You're a positive disgrace.

'We need your help to get the cart
Upright and on the road.'
'Poop, oh poop, oh stirring sight.'
Was all they heard from Toad.

'The only way to travel –
What poetry in motion!
A village skipped, a township jumped –
And causing such commotion.

'Oh poop, oh poop, oh my, oh my…
To think I never knew.'
'Don't be an ass,' the Mole cried out,
'Or I'll get mad with you.'

'Oh what dust clouds shall spring up
As I speed on my way;
And when a cart falls in a ditch,
Well, that will make my day.'

'What's to do with him?' asked Mole.
'Toad seems to think it's fun.'
'Nothing at all,' replied the Rat.
'There's nothing can be done.

'Silly Toad is now possessed
By yet another craze;
It always takes him in this way
In the initial phase.'

They checked the lovely cart once more
All smashed, just lying there.
They both felt very sorry, though
Daft Toad seemed not to care.

'Let's get on,' said Rat to Mole,
'And find the nearest town.
If we start now we should arrive
Before the sun goes down.'

'And what of Toad?' enquired the Mole.
'We can't just leave him here.'
'Bother Toad, I've done with him,'
The Rat said with a sneer.

But then dazed Toad caught up with them
And linked his arms in theirs;
He wore a blank expression and
He seemed quite free of cares.

'Now look here, Toad,' Rat sharply said,
He wore his fiercest frown,
'We're going off to see the police
The moment we reach town.

'We'll find a local blacksmith
To set the caravan right,
Then jump onto the first fast train
So we get home tonight.'

'See the police, repair the cart?'
Toad murmured, 'Don't you see!
I've done with carts forever –
I've seen the thing for me.

'What a heavenly vision, Rat!
Oh, I've been born anew.
And, dear Ratty, Mr Mole,
I owe it all to you.

'If you had never come along
To aid my little scheme,
I would have missed that stirring sight,
That car, that swan, that dream.'

'See what I mean,' remarked the Rat,
'He's really quite insane.
I'll never go a-pleasuring
With stupid Toad again.'

On reaching town they made quite sure
The horse was in good care,
Then found the railway station
And bought their homeward fare.

So it was very late that night
When they drew near Toad Hall;
They had to carry Toad back home
As he wouldn't walk at all.

Then Rat and Mole rowed homewards
Beneath the twinkling stars;
They both forgot the silly Toad
And speeding motor cars.

Once home they had some supper,
And, once again content,
Rat said, 'I'm glad that's over –
The worst days I've ever spent.'

'It's done with now,' replied the Mole.
He yawned and bowed his head;
'It's getting very late dear Rat,
Let's get ourselves to bed.'

~ ~ ~

Rat and Mole assumed the Toad
Would find good sense once more,
That he'd behave and settle down,
His lesson learnt for sure.

Next day, however, news was rife
With animals near and far,
The Toad had been to town to buy
A large, expensive car!

A hundred pairs of staring eyes
Gazed at him through the dark

THE WILD WOOD

'I'd like to meet the Badger,'
The Mole was heard to say.
'Be patient,' Rat then answered,
'He'll drop by one day.'

'Can't we ask him for a meal?'
Responded curious Mole.
'He wouldn't come,' said Rat, 'for he's
An antisocial soul.'

Mole scratched his head and said at last,
'I've had a great idea,
Why don't we go and visit him?
He lives quite close to here.'

'Just bide your time,' replied the Rat,
'You'll meet him by and by.
You must remember, my young friend,
Old Badger's very shy.

'I never call on him myself
Although I know him well;
Badger picks his own sweet time
To venture from his shell.

'Besides it's just not possible
Even if I thought we should,
For Badger lives deep in the heart
Of the perilous Wild Wood.'

'What if he does?' the Mole replied.
'You said it was safe, you know.'
'I know I did,' responded Rat,
'But it's not the place to go.'

With this Mole had to be content,
For Rat just held his ground;
And Badger, through those summer days
Just never came around.

The summer passed to autumn,
Then cold, dark winter came,
And still Mole thought of Badger,
With thoughts that stayed the same.

Rat would snooze for many hours,
(As Rats do in winter time)
Waking only now and then
To pen a simple rhyme.

But then on one dull, dreary day
Mole opened Rat's front door,
And headed for the Wild Wood
Determined to explore.

The sky was grey above him,
The weather bleak and cold,
But Mole strode out with daring,
His bearing brave and bold.

The world was deep in slumber,
The country stripped and bare,
But Mole found that he liked this scene
And walked without a care;

And with a cheerful spirit
He strode towards the Wood;
Rat's warnings of its dangers
He never understood.

The Wood lay there and looked just like
A black reef in a sea,
But as he entered it he said,
'This will not frighten me.'

Logs tripped him as he wandered,
Twigs crackled 'neath his feet,
The place was strange and eerie but
Mole found it quite a treat.

He penetrated further
To where the light was dim,
And all was still and silent
As dusk advanced on him.

The night soon gathered all around,
It overtook the day,
The light grew dim and dimmer
And then it drained away.

And then the faces started,
All indistinct at first:
The Mole who'd been so fearless, now
Began to fear the worst.

Wedge-shaped and very tiny
And evil to behold;
Scared Mole soon wished he'd stayed at home
And hadn't been so bold.

And then the faces disappeared
When frightened Mole turned round;
He found he stared at darkness –
Heard not the slightest sound.

He scarcely could believe he'd seen
A single hostile face;
He thought, 'I must be seeing things!'
As he increased his pace.

He passed another opening –
Was his sight telling lies?
Or did he see a narrow face
With cruel and evil eyes?

Then suddenly he saw them –
He knew he wasn't wrong.
They were clear for him to see;
They'd been there all along.

A hundred pairs of staring eyes
Gazed at him through the dark,
All filled with hate and malice and
A really evil spark.

Swinging off the path he ran
As quickly as he could,
Through untrodden places of
The horrible Wild Wood.

And then he heard the whistling,
From right behind at first.
Then frightened Mole ran on until
He thought his lungs would burst.

Again the whistling sounded.
This time from far ahead.
Now should he carry on, he thought
Or hurry back instead?

But while he was deciding
It broke out on either side,
Up and down and through and through
The dark Wood far and wide.

He was unarmed and all alone
Amongst the deathly din,
Far away from any help
And night was closing in.

Then the pattering began –
A weird and crazy sound;
At first he took the noise to be
Leaves falling to the ground.

Then it took a steady beat
And though he couldn't see,
He knew the pat, pat, pat of paws
Was all the sound could be.

The Mole stood still and listened –
His heart was filled with fear;
Then he heard a creature running,
And it was drawing near.

He thought the pace might slacken;
Transfixed he stood and gasped:
He saw a rabbit rushing by –
As it shot past it rasped,

'Get out of this, you silly fool!
Get out, I'm telling you.'
Then it rushed on through the Wood
And disappeared from view.

And then the pattering increased:
The Wood was running now,
Running fast and chasing hard;
It made a fearsome row.

For they were hunting someone
And they were closing in.
Mole had no doubt that they were out
To get his velvet skin.

Frightened, he began to run
As though he'd sprouted wings;
He ran and dodged and darted but
Kept falling over things.

He tried to find a place to hide,
Somewhere they wouldn't see;
At last he saw the perfect spot –
The hollow of a tree.

And deep within the hollow,
With all the noise outside,
He felt so sorry for himself
He very nearly cried.

For now he knew for certain
The terror of the Wood,
The terror that his friend, the Rat
Had known and understood.

~ ~ ~

Meanwhile the Rat was dozing
Amongst all he could desire,
Curled up within a comfy chair
Before a roaring fire.

A log then tumbled from the grate,
Crackled and spurted flame;
It made him wake up with a start,
Then sleep no longer came.

He reached out for his verses
Lying on the floor,
Thinking he would now attempt
To write a little more.

Then finding he was stuck for words
He shifted in his chair,
To ask the Mole for help – but found
No friendly Mole was there.

He called out and receiving
No answer to his call,
He raised himself and tottered
From his chair into the hall.

He found the Mole's galoshes
Were nowhere to be seen;
His hat was also missing from
The peg where it had been.

Rat ventured from his cosy home
To take a look around.
He saw the Mole's tracks clearly
Upon the frosty ground.

And they were running straight and true…
And then he understood:
The silly Mole had taken off
Towards the dark Wild Wood.

At this he looked both grave and stern,
Then went inside in haste;
He placed a pair of pistols in
A belt around his waist.

He grabbed a fearsome cudgel from
A corner of the hall,
Then straightened up and stood erect
To make himself look tall.

As dusk began to settle
He set off, a worried soul,
Courageous and determined now
To find his friend the Mole.

He reached the Wild Wood finally
As dusk fell all about.
He summoned up his courage
And pushed his small chin out.

And then he plunged into the Wood
To seek some sign of Mole;
Here and there a wicked face
Would pop up from a hole.

But seeing Rat was so well armed
They disappeared from view;
The whistling and the pattering
Fell silent quickly too.

So patiently Rat looked around
And called and called again,
Until he felt his weary search
Would be, alas, in vain.

Just when it seemed he'd lost all hope
He heard a voice quite near.
'Rat!' he heard the Mole cry out.
'Oh Rat, I'm over here.'

Mole's voice led Rat up to a tree
And there was Mole inside.
'Oh Rat, I've been so frightened.'
'You're safe now,' Rat replied.

'You've been a very silly Mole –
We river-bankers know
Far better than to enter here:
It's not a place to go.

'I did my best to warn you –
We don't come here alone.
Only Badger and bold Otter
Would come here on their own.'

'Surely Mr Toad would come?'
Mole queried from the tree.
'Old Toad come here?' the Rat replied,
And laughed out merrily.

'Toad wouldn't come through here alone,
Not in a hundred years.'
Rat laughed until his body shook –
His eyes filled up with tears.

Poor Mole was greatly cheered to see
His friend display such mirth,
And also very heartened by
The weapons round Rat's girth.

'Now we must make a start for home,'
Said Rat in worried tone,
'For this is not the place for us
To spend the night alone.'

'I'm very sorry,' said the Mole,
'For I don't mean to slack,
But could we have a little rest
Before we head on back?'

The Rat agreed and Mole lay down
To rest a little more;
His friend sat waiting patiently,
A pistol in each paw.

Finally the Mole woke up,
Much better for his doze;
He felt refreshed and warmer from
His head down to his toes.

'Now look what's happened,' said the Rat;
He wore a solemn frown.
'What's up?' enquired the Mole – said Rat,
'There's nothing up – it's down!

'Look, it's snowing hard out here;
Oh dear, this is a blow!
Of all the things to happen Mole,
It has to go and snow.

'But we must make a start,' said Rat.
'Head back the way we came.
It won't be easy now because
The Wood all looks the same.'

It wasn't easy either;
As always, Rat was right:
For now the Wood was covered in
A ghostly cloak of white.

They crossed the snowy footways,
Went round and then crisscrossed,
Till, weary and dispirited
They knew that they were lost.

Aching with fatigue they were
And bruised from where they'd tumbled.
'Is there no end to this vile Wood?'
Mole petulantly grumbled.

They rested till the Rat declared,
'Let's now push on anew,
For if we don't the snow will be
Too deep to battle through.'

And so once more they pressed ahead
But struggling through a dell,
The Mole tripped over something sharp
And, crying out, he fell.

'Oh, my poor leg!' he moaned in pain.
'Please wait, I'm all done in.
I don't think I can walk, dear Rat –
I've really hurt my shin.

'I must have tripped upon a branch.
It's really finished me.'
'There, there,' said Rat with kindness.
'Sit back and let me see.

'This was done with something sharp;
The cut is very clean.'
Rat pondered, then looked closely at
The spot where Mole had been.

'Never mind what did it Rat,'
Said Mole in quite some pain.
'It hurts most terribly and is
An awful cut and sprain.'

Rat was scratching busily
And scraping in the snow.
'Come off it, Rat,' admonished Mole,
'I'm in great pain, you know.'

Then suddenly Rat cried, 'Hooray!'
'What have you found?' asked Mole.
'This really isn't quite the time
To start to dig a hole.'

'Come and see,' Rat cried as he
Danced a merry caper.
Mole slowly hopped across and saw
A rusty old boot scraper.

'Well, what of it?' he crossly asked.
'It's a common thing to see.'
'But can't you see just what this means?'
Rat shouted out with glee.

'I just don't understand,' said Mole.
'What has got into you?
It's only just a scraper – and
A shabby old one too.'

'Just you get digging,' Rat replied;
'We'll soon be warm and dry.'
The Mole fell to indignantly
And gave a dismal sigh.

So both of them dug hard and fast
With each and every paw
Until they saw revealed at last
A large and solid door.

A bell-pull dangled at the side;
Near it a small brass plate,
And written there were two short words
That could transform their fate.

MR BADGER read the sign.
'You're a wonder, Rat,' said Mole.
'How very wise you are, dear Rat,
A truly clever soul.'

'Don't just sit there,' said the Rat.
'We must create a clamour,
Go and ring the doorbell hard
While I set to and hammer.'

Mole began to pull the bell,
His mind now free of care,
He pulled so hard he left the ground,
Feet swinging in the air.

The Rat was hammering loudly –
They both began to shout,
And then from far away they heard
A clanging bell ring out.

They warmed up by the roaring fire

MR BADGER

At last they heard another sound,
Of footsteps from inside;
The shuffling tread of slippers that
Were far too big and wide.

They heard a heavy bolt pulled back;
The door opened – just a trace;
A quivering snout and sleepy eyes
Peered from an angry face.

'Who is it now?' a voice complained.
'Speak up – I want to know.'
'It's us dear Badger,' Rat cried out.
'Lost in this beastly snow.'

'Ratty, my reckless little chap!'
The Badger changed his tone.
'This really is an awful night
To be out there alone.

'Come in at once, the pair of you.'
'Oh thank you,' they both cried.
They bumped into each other in
Their haste to get inside.

The Badger wore a dressing gown –
He'd risen from his bed –
But gave a hearty welcome as
He tapped them on the head.

'This is no night,' the Badger sighed,
'To be out roaming free.
Have you been up to mischief, Rat?
You'll be the death of me.'

He shuffled on in front of them
In slippers down at heel.
'I've a first rate fire going and
I bet you'd like a meal.'

They passed through endless tunnels
On an uneven floor,
Until the Badger opened up
A massive, wooden door.

A kitchen lay before them
With warm, inviting glow;
Badger ushered them inside
With a friendly, 'In you go.'

High-backed settles faced the fire,
Logs burned in Badger's grate,
It looked so warm and cosy –
In fact, it looked first rate.

They warmed up by the roaring fire,
Now over their ordeal,
Then sat at Badger's table to
Enjoy a tasty meal.

When they had finished eating,
Belts tight against their skin,
They felt content and carefree –
Both wore a happy grin.

They gathered round the embers
Of Badger's glowing grate,
And thought just what a treat it was
Sitting up so late.

'How's old Toad?' the Badger asked
In his kind, hearty way.
'You know I haven't seen him
For many a long day.'

'Oh, from bad to worse,' said Rat,
A grave look on his face.
'The way he drives his car is quite
A positive disgrace.

'Just last week another crash –
The car completely rolled.
Toad is lucky he's alive,
At least that's what I'm told.

'If only he would give it up
Or get a man to drive;
He's such a stubborn fool, I fear
Some days – he won't survive.'

'How many has he been through now?'
Asked Badger gloomily.
'Well – accidents or cars?' said Rat.
'But it's the same you see.

'I think this is the seventh;
The other six he crashed,
They're piled up on his coach-house roof,
All bent – completely smashed.'

'Hospitals too,' put in the Mole.
'He's been in lots of times,
And paid out loads of money for
His many traffic crimes.'

'And that's the trouble,' Rat went on.
'Toad's rich, we know for sure,
But he is not a millionaire
And can't ignore the law.

'And he could kill or maim someone
Before this fad is through;
Badger, we're his closest friends –
Whatever can we do?'

'Nothing at all,' the Badger said,
'And you both know the reason,
For this is not the kind of task
That suits the winter season.

'Once the year has really turned
We'll all take Toad in hand;
We'll sort his bad behaviour –
Oh yes – we'll make a stand.

'You're sleeping, Rat,' said Badger.
'Not me,' the Rat replied.
Mole and Badger laughed out loud –
They knew the Rat had lied.

'Well, now it's time we went to bed,'
Said Badger in his way.
'I'll take you to your quarters for
It's very nearly day.'

~ ~ ~

When late next morning, Rat and Mole
Rose from their comfy beds,
They found two little hedgehogs who
Stood up and ducked their heads.

'Finish off your meal,' said Rat.
'Sit down, sit down I say.
Where have you youngsters come from?
I'm sure you've lost your way.'

'Yes, please sir,' said the elder.
'We got lost in the snow.
And we went round and round and round,
Not knowing where to go.

'But then we stumbled up against
The Badger's friendly door
And knowing we were safe, we ceased
To worry any more.

'Mr Badger's very kind,
As everybody knows,
And we are not the first, for sure
He's rescued from the snows.'

Rat nodded and then asked them
If Badger was around.
'He went into his study, sir,
And said "Don't make a sound".

'He said he mustn't be disturbed
For he's got lots to do.'
Rat and Mole smiled knowingly
Because of course they knew…

That Badger was now fast asleep
Deep in his private lair,
A 'kerchief spread across his face
And snuggled in his chair.

The doorbell clanged out loudly,
Rat bade a hedgehog go.
He thought that someone else was lost
In the unexpected snow.

He soon returned with Otter
Who wore a smiling face.
The Otter gave his old friend Rat
A friendly, warm embrace.

'Get off me,' cried the Rat. 'Get off!'
His mouth was full of food.
'What in the world has put you
In such a boisterous mood?'

'Thought you'd be here,' the Otter said,
'Quite safe from any harm.
All along the river bank
You've caused such great alarm.

'Rat and Mole have disappeared,
They've not been home all night.
You've given all your closest friends
A monumental fright.

'But I knew where to find you –
It really was quite clear:
When creatures get in trouble, well,
They seem to end up here.

'They mostly go to Badger,
Or Badger gets to know,
So I came here directly
Through all this wretched snow.

'And as I hurried through the Wood
To see if all was well,
I came upon a rabbit
Just sitting in a dell.

'Oh, he was looking pretty brave –
I've seldom seen one bolder –
That was until I sidled up
And grabbed him by the shoulder.

'I asked him if he'd seen the Mole,
And if so, where he'd been;
I had to cuff him so he'd tell
Exactly what he'd seen.

'And so he told me everything –
(I gave him such a fright)
He told me that he'd seen scared Mole
In the Wood, last night.

'The whole Wild Wood was saying how
The Mole, Rat's special friend,
Was in a fix and heading for
A really nasty end.

'The Wooders, they were out about,
Chivvying him around,
And all four corners of the Wood
Filled with the awful sound.

' "You didn't try to help?" says I,
Cuffing him again.
"What me?" he said, "Do something! Me?
D'you think that I'm insane?" '

'Weren't you scared?' asked nervous Mole.
'Scared?' said he with glee.
'I'd give 'em nerves, if they should try
Anything on with me.'

Then Otter and the Rat sat down
To talk of river shop;
Only Badger coming in
Caused the pair to stop.

Badger rubbed his eyes and yawned –
Said in his kindly way,
'You must be worn out Otter,
Perhaps you'd like to stay?

'I'm sure you must be hungry and
Would like a bite to eat;
Please stay a while and join us;
I have a joint of meat.'

As Rat and Otter talked away
About Toad's latest car,
The Mole said, 'Down here Badger,
You know just where you are.

'It all feels so like home to me
For I have always found
I feel so safe and so secure
When I'm well underground.'

Badger simply beamed on him.
'Exactly what I say.
I can't feel safe and happy
Unless I live this way.

'And if your plans get larger,
You're wanting to expand,
You never have to wheel and deal
To buy some extra land.

'You simply dig and scrooge and scrape,
And there's a home for you,
And if it grows to be too large
You fill a hole or two.

'Now look at Rat – what does he do
If he should have a flood?
He has to move to somewhere else
Until he's free of mud.

'And then there's Toad – although I say
No word against Toad Hall –
But what if fire breaks out one day
Or tiles decide to fall?

'No – up above and out of doors
Is very good to roam,
But living here, safe underground,
Well – that's what I call home.'

The two henceforth became firm friends;
On all things they'd agree,
Badger said Mole understood
How home should really be.

'Now in a while,' the Badger said,
'You'll have a chance to dine,
Then afterwards I'll take you round
This splendid home of mine.'

And so a little later on
When they had had their meals,
As Rat and Otter settled down
To talk about some eels…

Badger took a lantern and
Mole followed him with care,
For a special guided tour
Of Badger's rambling lair.

They passed through endless tunnels in
The lantern's wavering light;
Mole marvelled at the many rooms
Off to the left and right.

He looked around with wonder,
Not trusting his own eyes;
He found it all amazing,
He was staggered by the size.

'However did you build it?
Clear all the mud and grime.
Where did you find the energy,
Let alone the time?'

'It would be quite amazing,'
Badger said with modest tone,
'But I did none of it you see –
You couldn't on your own.

'As far as I had need I cleared
Some of the chambers out;
And there are many more of them,
Around us and about.

'I see you do not understand,
So let me make it clear;
Years ago a city stood
Upon this land right here.

'It was a human city
And they were rich and clever.
They built a place to live, convinced
That it would last forever.'

'What became of them?' asked Mole.
'Well that we'll never know;
They live and build and flourish,
Stay awhile – then go.

'But badgers always lived here
Before the city came,
And now once more we badgers
Have come to stake our claim.

'When the people moved away
To build another town,
Animals came and liked it and
Began to settle down.

'They don't waste time in worrying
If men will come again.
The Wood now has its good and bad –
They're all right in the main.

'But you know something of them from
The happenings of last night.'
'Indeed I do,' replied the Mole
Quivering with fright.

'Not to worry,' Badger said.
'One day I'm sure you'll see,
That none of them are really bad;
So we should let them be.

'But I shall pass the word around
To creatures far and nigh;
Mole walks where he likes, or they
Must give me reason why.'

They came back to the kitchen
Where Rat paced up and down;
He looked annoyed and restless
And wore a sombre frown.

He had his overcoat pulled on,
His pistols in his belt.
'Come on, let's go,' he said to Mole,
Not hiding how he felt.

'We can't risk being stranded
For another night;
We must get going straightaway
While there is still some light.'

'Don't worry,' said the Otter,
'I'm coming too and know
Each and every woodland path
Down which we need to go.'

'You really needn't worry,'
Sighed Badger placidly.
'Just relax, the three of you,
Leave everything to me.

'My tunnels run much further
Than you all think they do;
I've bolt holes to the Wild Wood's edge
That you can journey through.'

But Rat was still most anxious
To be off and on his way;
He wished to see his river bank
Before the close of day.

So Badger took a lantern
And bade them follow him;
He led the way through tunnels
All damp and dark and dim.

They walked along bleak passageways
That dipped and dived and wound;
And some were hewn from solid rock
Devoid of any sound.

At last they saw some daylight
And then the passage end;
Badger bade them all goodbye –
They thanked their faithful friend;

And then he quickly disappeared,
As only Badger could,
And when they looked they found themselves
Beyond the dark Wild Wood.

Then all-knowing Otter said,
'Let's form a single file,
And make our way across that field
Towards the distant stile.'

They reached the stile and pausing
A moment to look back,
They saw the massive Wild Wood,
Dense, menacing and black.

And then they hurried on as if
Their legs had sprouted wings,
For home and hearth and firelight
And safe and pleasant things.

It seemed he now regretted
This sad and sorry mess

MR TOAD

All along the river bank
Summer had shown its face;
The bank had come alive again –
Resumed its normal pace.

Rat and Mole rose with the dawn
Keen to enjoy Rat's boat,
For Mole now shared his passion for
Those wooden things that float.

One day just after breakfast
When they could eat no more,
There came a thunderous hammering
At the Rat's front door.

'See who it is,' said Rat to Mole,
'Like the sport you are.'
Mole flung the door wide open and
Rat heard him cry, 'Hurrah!'

Mole shouted with excitement
As he ran down the hall.
He cried out, 'Mr Badger,
Has come to pay a call.'

This was wonderful indeed.
Remarkable to see,
For usually Badger only came
If needed urgently.

Badger stormed into the room
At a frantic pace;
He wore a stern expression on
His sharp and stripy face.

'The hour has come!' – 'What hour is that?'
The Rat asked nervously,
While glancing at the clock to check
Just what the hour could be.

'Whose hour? – you should rather say.
The hour of Toad, of course;
To take the silly fool in hand,
Perhaps by using force.'

'Toad's hour, of course,' piped up the Mole.
'Yes, I remember now.
We'll knock some sense into his head –
Oh Badger, tell us how.'

'I heard this morning,' Badger said,
'From a most worthy source,
That Toad received another car –
It's powerful, of course.

'And at this very moment
I've every cause to fear
That Toad is busy dressing in
His silly, driving gear.

'Into those clothes that turn him from
A pleasant looking Toad,
Into a being only fit
To terrorise the road;

'Into a stupid creature
That all have come to hate.
We must be up and doing
Before it is too late.

'The pair of you must come at once,'
Said Badger in stern tone,
'To Toad Hall where we'll sort him out;
I can't do it alone.'

'Right you are then,' Rat cried out,
'We're ready, aren't we, Mole?
We'll do everything to help
That poor misguided soul.'

So stern-browed Badger led the way
As they went down the road,
All three of them determined to
Convert the wayward Toad.

They reached Toad Hall quite quickly,
It wasn't very far,
And on arriving found outside
A shining motor car.

It stood before the massive house,
A gleaming shade of red.
Toad appeared as they approached.
'Hello, you chaps,' he said.

He swaggered down the broad front steps,
A scarf tied round his throat;
He wore a cap and goggles and
The most enormous coat.

'Come along, you fellows,'
He shouted out with glee.
'You've arrived in perfect time
To take a jaunt with me.

'We'll have a jolly, little…'
His words faded quite away
When he beheld the solemn looks
His friends all wore today.

'Get inside,' the Badger said.
'We're not playing any more.'
They dragged vexed Toad right up the steps
And pushed him through the door.

'Now first of all,' said Badger
With his stern eye on Toad,
'You cannot be allowed to cause
More havoc on the road.

'And take off all those silly things
And start to act your age.'
'Shan't,' said Toad with spirit.
'This is a gross outrage.

'I want an explanation.'
Badger ignored each word.
'Take them off him then,' he said,
As if he hadn't heard.

They laid Toad on the floor although
He kicked and called them names;
Then taking off his gear they said,
'We're not playing games.'

Now by this time Toad's anger
Had almost disappeared;
He no longer felt he was
A driver to be feared.

He was simply Toad and in
A tricky situation.
'You knew that it must come to this,'
Was Badger's explanation.

'You've ignored our constant warnings,
Thinking they're all funny.
You've earned yourself an awful name
And thrown away your money.

'In some ways you're a decent chap;
I hate to punish you,
But there's a limit Toad, you know
To what we'll let you do.

'We'll go into the smoking room
And there I'll have my say,
And then we'll see if you can be
Much better from today.'

He led Toad firmly by the arm,
(The Toad was in a swoon)
'That will do no good,' said Rat.
'Talk won't change his tune.

'He'll say just anything he can
To make things right in there;
It is a total waste of time –
Old Badger should beware.'

They heard the Badger's angry voice,
They heard it rise and fall,
Although exactly what he said
They couldn't tell at all.

Presently they heard the sobs
Of Toad in deep distress.
It seemed he now regretted
This sad and sorry mess.

Eventually the Badger
Opened up the door,
And then he solemnly came out
And coaxed Toad with his paw.

Then, limp and quite dejected,
His face an ashen hue,
His cheeks all wet from crying
Toad tottered into view.

'Now, now,' said Badger kindly
Pointing to a chair.
'Come on and be a good lad, Toad,
And sit down over there.

'My friends, I'm pleased to say that Toad's
Repented now at last;
He says he's truly sorry for
His conduct in the past.

'He says he'll give up driving;
This is understood.
I have his solemn promise,
It's final and for good.'

'Oh, what splendid news,' the Mole
Exclaimed from where he sat.
'Excellent news indeed,' observed
The unsure, doubting Rat.

He was looking hard at Toad,
Convinced he could espy
Something like a twinkle in
The Toad's still tearful eye.

'There's only one more thing to do,'
Said Badger pleasantly.
'Toad, I want you to repeat
What you just said to me.

'First you must say sorry for
The folly of your way.'
They all stood waiting patiently
To hear what Toad would say.

At last he spoke – defiantly.
He stood up very tall:
'It wasn't folly, Badger,
I'm not sorry – not at all.

'It was simply glorious –
Best fun I've ever had.
I can't say I regret it, though
You say that I've been bad.'

'What!' cried Badger scandalised.
He jumped up from his chair.
'You bad, backsliding animal –
I thought you said in there…'

'Oh yes, in there,' Toad shouted,
'When you went on at me,
I'd have said just anything,
For Badger you can be…

'So moving and so eloquent
And speak with such a ring,
But I've been searching through my mind,
Reviewing everything.

'And I am not repentant;
It was a clever sham.
So what on earth can be the sense
In saying that I am?'

'So you won't keep the promise which
You freely gave to me.'
'Quite the reverse, for I will drive
The first car that I see.

'Poop, poop – and off I'll go at speed,
And Badger, that is that.'
'I told you talk would do no good,'
Observed the scornful Rat.

'Very well,' said Badger,
'We'll try a different course;
Since we can't persuade you,
We must resort to force.

'I feared that it would come to this;
So here is what we'll do.
Many times you've asked us three
To come and stay with you.

'So we'll accept your offer
Until you mend your way.
We will not leave until we're sure
You mean just what you say.'

'It's for the best,' declared the Rat,
Pulling Toad upstairs.
'We'll attend to everything
And handle your affairs.

'Once you're fit and well we'll laugh
Just as we used to do,
But until that day arrives
We're taking charge of you.

'No more problems with the law;
No more bossy nurses.'
Rat made his way downstairs pursued
By angry Toad's loud curses.

'I'm sure this won't be easy,'
Said wise Badger sighing.
Rat and Mole of course both knew
That Badger wasn't lying.

'I've never seen old Toad so set,
But this is what we'll do:
We'll have to guard him day and night
And see the whole thing through.'

So they took turns to guard Toad's room
Throughout the hours of light;
Then each one took a turn to sleep
Within Toad's room at night.

At first he was most trying:
Made cars from bedroom chairs;
And then he'd crouch and look around
With silly fearsome stares.

Then he'd make ghastly noises,
And when he'd done, he cried,
Tipped all the chairs upon the floor
As if quite satisfied.

And then he'd do it all again,
And then, when he was done,
Well, off he'd go once more, it seemed,
He found the whole thing fun.

As time went by, however,
These noisy tantrums died;
His interest in the world outside
Went on a downward slide.

And then one morning, Rat, whose turn
It was to guard the Toad,
Came to relieve the Badger
From his irksome load.

'Toad's still in bed,' said Badger.
'He isn't feeling well;
He says it might pass off in time –
Or won't – he just can't tell.

'Now you be very careful, Rat.
For there's one thing I know:
The Toad is full of artfulness
When acting the hero.'

So Rat approached Toad's bedside.
'How are you now, old chap?'
He had to wait some minutes while
Toad surfaced from his nap.

At last Toad's voice responded.
It sounded weak and tired.
'Thank you very much, dear Rat –
So nice that you enquired.

'But tell me how you are yourself
And that good chap, the Mole?'
'Oh we're just fine,' Rat said, convinced
Toad was an honest soul.

'Mole's gone off with Badger
Enjoying this fine weather,
So we will spend a pleasant day –
Just you and me together.

'Now Toad – jump up old fellow.
Don't mope around in there.'
'Oh, dear kind Rat,' replied the Toad,
'I know you really care.

'But I am far from jumping up,
I fear I'll not get stronger;
I hate to be a burden – but
I won't be for much longer.

'Indeed, dear Rat – I hope I won't.'
Said Rat, 'That pleases me.
You've been a bother to us all,
I'm sure you must agree.

'I'm glad it's going to stop at last
With weather such as this.
Do you know the fun you've caused
The three of us to miss?'

'I am a trouble,' uttered Toad,
'And I can clearly see
You must be really quite fed up
With looking after me.

'I mustn't ask another thing;
I'm a nuisance and that's plain.'
'I'd do anything,' said Rat
'To see you fit again.'

'If I thought that,' Toad softly said,
More feebly than before,
'I'd send you to the village
To do one favour more…

'To go and fetch the doctor…'
His voice was very hoarse,
'But no, it's too much trouble,
Let's let things take their course.'

'Why do you want a doctor?'
Rat viewed Toad's sagging skin;
He lay there flat and very still
And did look rather thin.

'You must have seen,' said Toad, 'how I've
Declined since yesterday;
But no, dear Rat – why should you?
Yet one day you will say…

' "If only I'd observed before
How ill poor Toad had been;
If only I had noticed,
If only I had seen." '

'Look here, old man,' replied the Rat,
His face concerned and set,
'I'll fetch a doctor for you, but
You can't be that bad yet.

'Let's talk of something else – cheer up...'
'I fear my friend,' said Toad,
'Talk can't do much in such a case
So far along the road.

'And doctors can't help either –
Or none I ever saw –
But still, at times like this, you know
You grasp the slightest straw.

'So maybe you are right, dear Rat,
If one is feeling weak,
The help of a good doctor
Is sensible to seek.

'And Rat, while you're about it,
As you'll pass by the door,
Please ask my lawyer to drop in
To do a little chore.

'It would be such a service:
Though I don't like to ask,
There comes a time one has to face
The most unpleasant task.'

'A lawyer! Well you must be bad
To talk such gloom and doom.'
Rat hurried off but first made sure
That he had locked the room.

Once outside he stopped to think,
'I have to go,' he said.
'I've never known old Toad to have
Such thoughts inside his head.

'I'd better keep him happy.
It won't take very long;
The doctor will assure him
He's got it all quite wrong.'

Once Rat had disappeared, old Toad
Laughed to himself and sighed,
'A clever ruse, without a doubt –
I took him for a ride.'

Then Toad hopped lightly out of bed,
Now very much alive;
He chuckled as the trusting Rat
Went off along the drive.

Toad then put on his smartest suit
As fast as he was able,
Then filled his pockets up with cash
From the bedside table.

Then with his bed-sheets knotted tight
He quickly tied them round
The mullion of the window and
Slipped lightly to the ground.

He laughed out loud with pride and joy
To find that he was free,
Then made his way along the drive
As happy as could be.

~ ~ ~

It was a tough old time for Rat
On his friends return.
They listened to his story
Both looking very stern.

When Badger spoke it sounded like
Rat's actions were a crime,
And then the Mole said ruefully,
'You let us down this time.'

'He did it awfully well,' said Rat.
'I wish that you'd been here.'
'He did you awfully well, you mean,'
Said Badger with a sneer.

'But talking won't help matters –
He's clear away by now –
And there is nothing to be gained
If we all start to row.

'Toad is such a big-head and
He'll think he's been so clever,
There's no telling what he'll do.
There's one good thing however…

'For we won't have to waste our time
And guard him any more,
Though we had better stay right here
As there's one thing for sure…

'He's bound to get in trouble,
It seems it's just his way,
And my good friends – although it's harsh –
Well, I am bound to say…

'He'll be brought back here at some time
By stretcher – or the law.'
Badger spoke not knowing what
The future had in store.

~ ~ ~

The carefree, happy Toad meanwhile
Was walking down the road.
'Smart piece of work,' he chuckled.
'Oh, what a clever Toad!

'It's merely just a case of brain
Matched against brute force;
And first-rate brain comes out on top.
It's bound to do, of course.

'Rat'll catch it from old Badger
About this situation;
He's such a worthy fellow too,
But just lacks education.

'I'll take the lad in hand,' thought Toad.
He walked devoid of care;
His mind was full of silly schemes,
His nose was in the air.

Presently he reached a town
And saw along a street
An inn – and this reminded him
That it was time to eat.

He'd missed his breakfast and was now
Hungry from his walk,
And so he marched into the inn
And ordered bread and pork.

Toad was just halfway through his meal
When he sat up and frowned…
Then trembled with excitement at
That oh-so-pleasant sound.

The poop, poop, poop drew nearer,
Toad found it very hard
To hide all his emotions as
The car stopped in the yard.

A party came into the room,
Jubilant and gay;
They talked about their motor car –
The pleasures of the day.

Toad sat and listened eagerly,
And then could wait no more;
He paid his bill and softly slipped
Out through the courtyard door.

'It can't do any harm to look.
Who could be offended?'
So spoke the Toad as he approached
The car, now unattended.

Slowly Toad walked round the car –
A lovely thing to see.
He mused and thought, 'You know it's just
As though it's here for me.'

And then, though hardly knowing how,
The crank was in his paw.
He turned it – passion seized him when
He heard the engine roar.

His very soul was mastered
In just one quick heartbeat,
Then with a leap he landed
Right in the driving seat.

He pushed the car's gear lever
And swung the wheel round hard,
Then drove the car off in a dream
At speed, across the yard.

And then out through the archway
And out onto the road,
And once again he felt fulfilled –
A very happy Toad.

He didn't care what happened,
No sense of right or wrong;
Feeling vibrant and alive
He quickly sped along.

~ ~ ~

The Magistrate looked sternly down,
Said he was of a mind
To give the toughest sentence
That he could ever find…

To the hardened ruffian
Cowering in the dock,
Who'd stolen a fine motor car
And driven it amok.

And who'd addressed a policeman
With gross impertinence;
He asked to know the harshest term
Laid down for this offence.

Without of course allowing
The benefit of doubt,
Because none could be given
To such a loathsome lout.

The Clerk of Court then scratched his nose
And presently observed,
That a good long stretch in prison
Was what the Toad deserved.

'Some people would consider
To steal a motor car
Was really quite the worst offence
Against the law by far.

'But cheeking policemen rightly has
The larger penalty.'
He scratched his nose again and said,
'Now then – let me see.

'I'd give him twelve months for the theft,
Which isn't very tough,
And three years for the driving,
Is quite lenient enough.

'And fifteen years then for the cheek
Which was pretty bad one fears.
Now adding up those figures
Makes exactly nineteen years.'

'Well done!' said the Magistrate
With a smile he couldn't hide.
'Make it twenty,' said the Clerk
'To be on safety's side.'

'An excellent suggestion,'
Said the Magistrate with glee.
'Toad, pull yourself together.
Stand up and look at me.

'It's time to pass your sentence,
So listen carefully Toad;
It's time you learnt your lesson for
Your terror on the road.

'Remember that the next time
You'll get far more – you'll see.
This time it will be twenty years
Before we set you free.'

Then many men came forward
And marched unhappy Toad,
Imploring and protesting
Along the busy road.

On across the market place,
Shouts ringing in his ears:
The hooting of school children –
The sound of grown-ups' jeers.

On into a castle
Unhappy Toad was led,
Across a creaking drawbridge
With towers overhead.

Past grinning soldiers coughing
In a horrid way;
Past mastiffs straining at the leash
Though keepers told them 'Stay.'

On down through endless stairways
(Poor Toad began to weep)
Until they reached the grimmest cell
Within the castle keep.

They came upon a jailer with
A jangling bunch of keys.
'Rouse up, old man! Take over,'
Said a warder with a wheeze.

'Take this vile and loathsome Toad
Of devious resource;
Watch him well with all your skill
For he shows no remorse.'

The jailer nodded grimly,
He took Toad by the arm;
A key creaked in an ancient lock
And caused the Toad alarm.

Poor Toad was thrown into a cell,
His spirits hit the floor;
He lay there shaking at the sound
Of the closing door.

He knew he was forgotten –
There'd be no helping hand –
Within the strongest castle keep
In England's merry land.

'I'll never be set free again'

TOAD'S ADVENTURES

When Toad found that a dungeon
Was now his new abode,
He cried aloud, 'This is the end
Of daring Mr Toad.

'The end of handsome Mr Toad,
Distinguished and so rare,
Toad so rich and popular,
So fine and debonair.

'I'll never be set free again
To see the light of day,
After stealing that fine car
In that audacious way:

'And for the most outrageous cheek –
A kind not seen before.'
But then his sobs made him collapse
Upon the dungeon floor.

'Now I must stay within this cell
Till those who called me friend,
Will just forget the name of Toad –
Oh what a sorry end.

'Oh wise old Rat and Badger
And sensible, good Mole,
If I had heeded what they said
I'd not be in this hole.'

With cries and moans and endless tears
He bore the days and nights,
Refusing all the prison meals
And all his other rights.

Now the jailer had a daughter
Who helped out with the chores;
And she was fond of animals
And loved the great outdoors.

This kind girl, feeling sorry for
The state poor Toad was in,
Told her father she abhorred
To see Toad grow so thin.

'Father, I can't bear to see
Toad getting low and sad,
Let me take good care of him,
I'll show you he's not bad.

'I'll make him eat out of my hand,
Sit up and take some food.'
'Well, take charge then,' he answered.
'I'm tired of Toad's bad mood.'

And so the young girl hurried off
And rapped on Toad's cell door.
'Come on – cheer up Toad,' she said,
'No crying any more.

'And do please try to eat some food.
I've brought you some of mine.'
But Toad refused it saying,
'I'm too depressed to dine.'

Bubble and squeak was on the plate,
Its sweet smell filled the cell,
But Toad refused to eat it
And said, 'I'm just not well.'

And so the wise girl let him be,
The smell though stayed behind.
Toad finally stopped sobbing,
Fresh thoughts sped through his mind...

Of chivalry and poetry,
Deeds waiting to be done;
Of meadows with cows grazing
Caressed by wind and sun.

Of gardens with herb borders,
Of bushes – swaying trees;
He thought of warm snapdragons
Visited by bees.

The clink of fine white dishes on
The table at Toad Hall,
How perfect everything had been
Before his hapless fall;

How if his friends knew of his fate
They'd set him free by force;
He thought of his great cleverness
And limitless resource.

He thought of how his restless mind
Was up to any feat –
And that was all it took then for
The cure to be complete.

Later when the girl returned
With toast and steaming tea,
Toad smelled the toast and thought of all
The times when he'd been free.

It talked of cosy kitchens,
Of hearths on winter's nights,
Of sitting up with slippered feet
Putting the world to rights.

So Toad sat upright once again,
Sipped tea and dried his eyes,
He talked a lot about himself
And how folk thought him wise.

He told her who he was – and too
About his ancient kin;
About his goings here and there –
The house that he lived in.

The young girl listened to him speak,
And watched him drink his tea.
'Tell me about Toad Hall,' she said,
'It sounds so grand to me.'

'My Toad Hall,' he said with pride
And mounting confidence,
'Is a stately, self contained
Historic residence.

'It dates from fourteen hundred,
A splendid house indeed,
And naturally it's fitted out
With everything I need:

'Modern sanitation,
Minutes from the store,
Close to the church and post office
And very handy for…'

'Why, bless the creature,' said the girl,
'I'm not buying it you know.
Tell me some real things of it,
But before you do I'll go…

'And fetch you some more tea and toast
Now you seem well today.'
She tripped away and soon returned
And with a laden tray.

Toad pitched into the toast with glee,
His spirits now restored.
He told her of his boathouse
Where all his boats were moored.

Of his walled kitchen garden,
About his pigsties too,
About the hen-house and the grounds,
A pleasure to walk through.

He told her of the dining hall,
Of fun when he'd been free;
He said, 'When I tell stories,
That's when I'm really me.'

And then she asked about his friends,
Wondering what he'd say.
He told her where they lived, and how
They passed the time of day.

So when she said goodnight to him,
Having shaken up his straw,
Toad had without a doubt become
His smug old self once more.

He sang a little song or two
Before settling down to rest.
Of course the songs all centred on
How he, the Toad, was best.

~ ~ ~

Now they had many varied talks
As the days passed by;
Often the jailer's daughter
Was heard to sadly sigh.

For she grew sorry for poor Toad
And thought it such a shame,
That this dear little creature,
Who really was quite tame...

Should be locked up in a prison
For such a small offence.
It really seemed to be unfair
And made so little sense.

But Toad in his big-headed way,
Thought her kindness nothing less —
Than she was overcome and with
A growing tenderness.

Of course, he rued the social gulf
Between them was so wide,
For she was very pretty and
Would make a worthy bride.

One day the girl was thoughtful,
Half-hearted with replies;
She just ignored the Toad's remarks
Which he believed were wise.

'Toad, listen for a moment,'
The girl then firmly said:
She whispered to the Toad as she
Gently bowed her head.

'My aunt's a washerwoman.'
'There, there, dear,' Toad replied.
'I have some aunts who ought to be.'
He sniggered as he lied.

'Be quiet for a minute.
You talk too much,' she said.
'And while I'm trying hard to think
Your talking hurts my head.

'Now as I said, I have an aunt,
She washes for the castle;
She takes it out on Mondays
Wrapped up in a parcel.

'She brings it back on Fridays –
This is Thursday, as you know –
Now this is what occurs to me:
You're rich – or say you're so.

'She's poor and a few sovereigns
Would not be missed by you,
But they would mean a lot to her
And help her to get through.

'I think if you approached her,
And "squared" her, as you'd say,
You might reach an agreement
To help you get away.

'She could let you have her dress,
Her bonnet and her cape;
Disguised then as a woman
You could make a bold escape.

'You're like her in so many ways,
Especially round the waist.'
'We're not alike,' Toad crossly said
With evident distaste.

'I have a pleasant figure
Whatever you may say.'
'So has my aunt,' the girl replied,
'But have it your own way.

'You're horrid and ungrateful;
I'm trying to get you free.'
'Yes, yes,' said Toad with feeling,
'I'm sorry, pardon me.

'But surely you would not expect
That Toad of fine Toad Hall,
Should dress up as a woman – well!
It wouldn't do at all.'

'Then you can stop here as a Toad,
A prisoner of the law.
It sounds as if you want to leave
In a coach and four.'

Now Toad was always ready
To admit when in the wrong.
'You're good and kind,' he said, 'and I've
Been stupid all along.

'Introduce me to your aunt
If you would be so kind,
And then I have no doubt at all
Together we will find…

'A sensible arrangement
To suit the pair of us;
We'll come to an agreement
With minimum of fuss.'

Next day the girl returned to Toad,
Her aunt came with her too;
The worthy woman had been briefed
Before the interview.

The sight of golden sovereigns
Dispensed with any fuss.
It settled things quite rapidly,
Left nothing to discuss.

Toad was given garments –
To see them made him frown –
An apron, shawl and bonnet
And printed, cotton gown.

The only thing the aunt desired
Was to be gagged and bound,
So she'd escape suspicion
When later she was found.

This suggestion pleased vain Toad
More than any in a while,
For it would mean that he could leave
In bold and daring style.

His reputation reaffirmed
As a smart, dashing chap,
A really glamorous villain
Whom no-one could entrap.

He helped the jailer's daughter
To make her aunt appear
The victim of a wild attack
That anyone would fear.

'It's your turn Toad, remove your coat,'
She said, 'And put it down.'
Then laughingly she dressed him up
In her aunt's old cotton gown.

As she arranged the woollen shawl
She couldn't hide a grin,
Nor when she tied the bonnet strings
Beneath Toad's sagging chin.

She laughed, 'You look just like her.
A laundress to be sure;
I'm convinced you've never looked
So respectable before.

'Now goodbye Toad and lots of luck,
Go back the way you came;
And if the men make fun of you,
Well, you make fun the same.'

Toad set out with quaking heart,
His mind a total bluster,
He took the firmest footsteps
He found that he could muster.

But he was very soon surprised,
Indeed most humbled too,
That the fondness for the aunt
Helped him in getting through.

Her figure clad in cotton print
That they so often saw,
Seemed to be a passport
For each forbidding door.

When he didn't know the way
And got into a state,
He found he was assisted by
The warders at a gate.

They joked and asked him questions
Which slowed his frantic haste;
Somehow he kept his temper whilst
Replying in good taste.

Then finally the last gate slammed
Loudly at his rear,
And when it did he knew for sure
He need no longer fear.

He headed for the lights of town,
Quite dizzy with success;
He knew he must get clear away
To seal his happiness:

For the aunt whose clothes he wore,
Whom everyone thought good,
Was liked, well-known and popular
Throughout the neighbourhood.

As he walked, lost in these thoughts
He saw a coloured light,
Then another – red and green;
This was a welcome sight.

And then he heard a puff and snort –
The shunting of a truck.
'Aha!' he thought, 'A railway –
This is a piece of luck.

'It is the thing I need the most,
And what is even more,
I needn't venture into town –
Risk trouble with the law.'

Toad headed for the station,
As fast as he was able,
And wasting not a moment –
He checked the train timetable.

He found a train was leaving,
And passing by Toad Hall.
It left within the hour and so
He'd hardly wait at all.

'More luck!' the Toad cried happily,
Now almost free of care.
He went up to the counter
To buy his homeward fare.

He asked for his home station,
Then fumbled for some money,
But when he searched his pockets –
He noticed something funny.

His waistcoat wasn't there.
His coat had gone as well.
He'd left them both behind – of course
In the prison cell.

Toad realised at once, but then
His next thought made him freeze,
For with them he had left behind
His money, watch and keys.

In panic he attempted still
To carry the whole thing off,
Assuming his old manner
Of country gent and toff.

'Good sir, I've left my purse behind
So will you let me borrow
A ticket now to get me home –
I'll pay you back tomorrow.

'I'm well known round these parts you know.'
'I'll bet,' the clerk replied,
'If you have tried this game before.
Now madam, stand aside.'

Then an old man prodded Toad
And said, 'Get out the way.'
He called him his 'good woman',
The worst insult that day.

Toad baffled and despairing,
Walked towards the train;
Tears trickled down his cheeks as he
Searched through his mind in vain.

How could he solve this problem?
It all had looked so fine,
And safety had been oh so close
Just down the railway line.

And then to have no money;
This really was too hard –
And then the pettifogging clerk
Of this rotten railway yard.

And soon they'd find that he'd escaped.
He must get on a train
Or he'd be caught and taken back
Bound in a heavy chain.

The girl would make such snide remarks,
She'd even think it fun;
He'd be on bread and water.
Whatever could be done?

He walked along the platform,
The train was being oiled,
And there he saw the driver
In clothes all black and soiled.

'Whatever's wrong?' the driver asked.
'Now you can talk to me.'
'Oh sir, I'm so upset,' cried Toad,
'As you can surely see.

'I've lost my every penny
And Lord alone knows where,
And I must get back home tonight
But I can't pay my fare.'

'Oh dear, oh dear,' the driver said,
'What a bad to-do!
And kids as well, I shouldn't doubt,
Who all depend on you.'

'Several of them,' sobbed the Toad.
'I've lots of kids, you see.
They'll all be misbehaving and
They'll all be missing me.'

'Tell you what I'll do,' he said.
'You wash, for which you're paid;
Well I'm an engine driver,
Which is a dirty trade.

'If you will wash some shirts for me,
I'll give you a free ride.'
'I will, I will, with loving care,'
Toad readily replied.

He thought, 'I'll send him money.
It is the selfsame thing.'
And then he jumped onto the train
With an almighty spring.

The guard then waved the chequered flag –
Toad's heart leapt with elation –
The big steam engine panted,
Then pulled out from the station.

Gradually the speed built up
And Toad could see at last
Tall trees and cows and hedges
As they went whizzing past.

He began to skip and shout
And carol bits of song;
He felt supremely happy as
The engine sped along.

They'd covered many a mile and Toad
Was planning what he'd eat,
When finally he reached Toad Hall –
He'd fix himself a treat.

But then he saw the driver's face
As he leant o'er the side;
He was listening very hard
And didn't try to hide…

The worry that he felt and said,
As he kept looking back,
'I thought we were the final train
Along this piece of track.

'And yet I could have sworn I heard
Another train back there.'
Poor Toad could not remember
Receiving such a scare.

The driver looked again, and then
He called above the row,
'I can see another train,
I see it clearly now.

'It looks as if we're being chased.
It's setting such a pace.'
The frightened Toad clasped both his paws
To his despairing face.

'It's carrying the strangest bunch
Of folk I ever saw.
Some look like the police – are you
In trouble with the law?'

Toad fell upon his knees and clasped
His paws in supplication.
'Oh help and save me, dear kind sir,'
He cried in desperation.

'I will confess it all – I'm not
The thing I seem to be.
I am a Toad who's managed
By daring to break free…

'From deep within a dungeon,
Ignored by everyone;
And if those fellows capture me,
You know what will be done?

'I'll be on bread and water
And locked behind a door,
And misery and heartache
Will plague the Toad once more.

'They'll leave me there to languish
In that awful cell,
Shivering in the cold and damp
That makes me feel unwell.'

The driver scrutinised poor Toad,
A fugitive from law.
'Tell me the truth,' he asked him then.
'What were you locked up for?'

'I borrowed someone's motor car –
It's such a little crime;
The owners who were lunching
Didn't need it at the time.'

The driver then looked very grave.
'You've been a wicked Toad;
By rights you ought to pay the price
For everything you've sowed.

'But I will not desert you
When you're in such distress,
So obviously in trouble
And in an awful mess.

'An animal that's suffering
Makes me feel quite queer;
So Toad, we still may beat them yet –
I'll get you out of here.'

They piled on lots and lots of coal,
The engine leapt ahead,
But presently the driver turned
Again to Toad and said,

'I'm afraid it's no good Toad.
Yours is a hopeless plight,
They have the better engine and
They're running very light.

'There's only one thing left right now
That we can try to do,
So listen very carefully
To what I'm telling you.

'There's a tunnel just ahead
And after that a wood;
In the tunnel they'll slow down –
As indeed we should.

'But I'll put on as big a head
Of steam as I can do;
Then I'll shut off the steam and brake,
The moment that we're through.

'Then just as soon as it is safe,
Jump quickly out and hide,
Then I'll put on full steam ahead
And lead them quite a ride.'

They piled on loads more coal until
The steam belched from the funnel;
The engine roared and rattled as
It shot into the tunnel.

When they shot out the other end
Into the moonlit night,
The driver shut off steam while Toad
Made ready to alight.

The train slowed down to walking pace;
Toad heard the driver yell,
'Jump out now and good luck Toad.'
He jumped and then he fell…

Down a short embankment,
He toppled, rolled and slid,
Then scrambling to his feet he dived
Into the wood and hid.

He peeped to see the engine
Build up its speed again,
Then bursting from the tunnel
He saw the other train.

The folk on board were shouting,
'Stop right away we say!'
Toad gave the heartiest laugh he'd had
In many a long day.

He stopped however, when he thought
About his situation,
For it was cold and he was gripped
With growing desperation.

For he was in an unknown wood –
No money and alone –
And with no chance of supper:
The thought made poor Toad groan.

The silence all around him
As he stood taking stock
Was really overpowering
And came as quite a shock.

He knew he shouldn't venture from
The shelter of the wood,
And yet he couldn't stay right there
Just rooted where he stood.

But after jail the wood seemed strange,
And though it was a whim,
He felt it was unfriendly and
Was poking fun at him.

A nightjar's eerie rattle
Came from the wood's far borders;
It made him think the trees were filled
With fearsome prison warders.

A tawny owl swooped down and brushed
His shoulder with its wing,
He thought it was a policeman's hand
Or some such horrid thing.

And then he met a fox who stopped
And looked him up and down.
'Washerwoman,' he laughed out,
'You're miles away from town.

'There's half a pair of socks astray
And two shirts short this week –
Mind it don't occur again.'
Toad was too mad to speak.

He hurried on and left the fox
Laughing merrily;
It was now growing very dark
Which made it hard to see.

But still he struggled gamely on,
Down lanes and over stiles,
Through fields and woods and meadows,
He covered many miles.

At long last, cold and hungry
He sheltered in a tree,
Slept soundly then till morning
Just thankful to be free.

'Tell me, do you want to sell
That mangy horse of yours?'

THE FURTHER ADVENTURES OF TOAD

Toad was awoken early
By sunlight streaming in;
He would have slept for longer –
With blankets to his chin.

But he was now awoken
By coldness in his feet;
Sitting up he looked around,
His heart then missed a beat.

For he remembered everything:
Escape, pursuit and flight,
And all the frantic happenings
Of the previous night.

But he remembered, best of all,
He was completely free;
How everything could now return
To how it used to be.

He shook himself and brushed away
Some brown, dry leaves, with care,
Then jumping from the tree strode off
With bold and buoyant air.

Though cold and tired and hungry
He still felt fit and fine,
His nightmare of the day before
Dispelled by warm sunshine.

Toad now looked out for someone who
Could point where he should head,
But there was just the empty road
Which cared not where it led.

Then presently a small canal
Came up along its side,
But it was silent like the road,
Just equally tongue-tied.

'Bother and drat them both,' said Toad,
'But one thing's surely clear:
They must have come from somewhere else
For them to end up here.

'I can sort this out,' he thought
Continuing his course;
Then walking round a bend he saw
A solitary horse.

A line hung round the horse's neck,
So Toad was keen to find
Just what the horse was up to,
And what he pulled behind.

Then with a swirl of water
Appeared a bright blue barge,
And sitting at the tiller was
A woman, stout and large.

'Nice morning, ma'am,' she called to Toad.
'Maybe for some,' Toad said.
'But not for those in trouble and
With problems in their head.

'My married daughter asks for me
And sends me urgent word,
So off I come not knowing what
Has possibly occurred.

'But naturally, I fear the worst
And don't know what to do,
As you will understand yourself
If you're a mother too.

'I'm in the washing business
As you can surely see,
And I have left my kids alone –
What imps they all can be.

'And I've lost all my money
And also lost my way,
So I'm borne down with worries!
It's such a dreadful day.'

'Where does your daughter live good ma'am?'
'By the river,' Toad replied.
'Close to a mansion called Toad Hall,
Set on the riverside.

'It's owned by Mr Toad, who's known
For wealth and his fine way.'
'Toad Hall, why yes I know it and
I'll pass by there today.

'This canal soon joins the river,
So come along with me;
You can come on board the barge
And keep me company.'

And so the woman steered the barge
Expertly to the side.
The grateful Toad stepped on and said,
'Thank you for the ride.'

As he sat down with great relief,
'Toad's luck again,' thought he;
'Right out there on top once more
Just as it's bound to be.'

'You wash clothes,' the woman said
As they now moved along.
'A worthy business too, I'm sure,
If I'm not far from wrong.'

'Finest of them all,' said Toad.
'It suits me to a T;
All the gentry round these parts
Put washing out with me.

'I'm the only one they'll use;
I understand my work:
Washing, ironing and the like,
They know I never shirk.'

'You don't do everything yourself?'
'Oh no!' Toad shook his head.
'I have a lot of girls to help –
Twenty or more,' he said.

'They're nasty little hussies.
It's true – they're nothing less.'
'I agree,' the woman said
With knowing heartiness.

'But are you fond of washing?'
Toad threw a rapturous fit.
'Fond of washing?' he replied.
'I simply dote on it.

'When both my arms are in a tub,
That's when I'm really me;
It's such a pleasure to me ma'am,
And it comes easily.'

'What good luck,' the woman said.
'Why?' Toad was heard to ask.
'Well, I like washing too,' she said.
'It's such a pleasant task…

'But my husband's very lazy,
I don't get a minute free,
He should really steer the barge
But leaves it all to me.

'He's gone hunting for a rabbit –
At least that's what he said –
And I've a pile of washing but
Must steer the barge instead.'

'Forget the washing,' Toad replied,
Turning the subject round.
'Just think of that young rabbit,
A fat one, I'll be bound.'

'I just think about my washing,
There is so much to do,
But I'm sure you'd be delighted
If I gave it all to you.

'Downstairs in the cabin
Are clothes all thick with grime,
If you will wash them through, why it
Will help to pass the time.

'You can put them in the tub
As we go on our way,
'Twill give you pleasure and, for sure,
Will really make my day.'

Unhappy Toad, he gasped aloud,
His stomach muscles tightened.
'Why not let me steer?' he said
Now feeling very frightened.

'Why, you might wash a different way.'
He tried to hide his fright.
'I might spoil your lovely things,
Not do them all quite right.

'I'm used to clothes for gentlemen.
It's where I really shine.
It's what I'm really used to.
They are my special line.'

'Let you steer!' the woman cried –
She laughed out heartily.
'No, it takes time to learn to steer
A barge like this you see.

'Besides, it's dull work steering,
Just sitting in this seat;
Don't take away my pleasure
In giving you a treat.

'No, you shall do the washing
At which you're a dab hand,
And I'll stick to the steering that
I know and understand.'

Toad was completely cornered
And in a dreadful state,
But sullenly accepted this
Distressing turn of fate.

'Now if it comes right down to it,'
He thought in desperation,
'Any fool can wash some clothes
With a little application.'

He filled the tub and fetched some soap
And settled down to work;
Poor Toad got cross and crosser
But knew he mustn't shirk.

Nothing that he tried to do
Did really any good;
He tried to coax and slap the clothes
And things he thought he should.

He got into an awful mess
As they were pulled along.
Everything he tried to do
Just kept on going wrong.

He looked towards the woman.
She looked the other way;
His back was aching badly and
He noticed with dismay…

His paws were getting crinkly,
They no longer looked so nice;
Toad muttered and then lost the soap
And cursed out once or twice.

A burst of rough, coarse laughter
Caused him to look around,
To see what had occasioned
Such an unpleasant sound.

It was the sturdy barge woman
Laughing merrily.
'I've been watching all the time,
And what a sight!' says she.

'I thought you must be lying
From your conceited way;
You've never washed a dishcloth,
Not in your life, I'll lay'

Toad's temper had been rising,
Now it boiled like cooking fat.
'You common, low down thing!' he cried.
'Don't talk to me like that.

'I am a most respected Toad
And one who's famous too;
I won't be ridiculed, d'you hear?
Not by the likes of you.'

'Why so you are,' she said with scorn.
'Well, what a fine to-do!
A horrid, nasty-looking Toad –
And on my nice barge too.

'Now that's a thing I just won't stand.'
Out shot a mottled arm;
It grabbed Toad's leg and gripped it though
He struggled in alarm.

She grabbed his other leg and then,
Confirming Toad's worst fears,
Everything turned upside down,
Wind whistled in his ears.

Then Toad flew swiftly through the air,
Spinning as he flew.
The water when he reached it – well!
It chilled him through and through.

He landed with a mighty splash;
He gave an angry roar;
On surfacing he looked around –
The first thing that he saw…

Was the brawny barge woman
Laughing fit to burst.
'I'll get revenge on you – I will!'
He coughed and choked and cursed.

Swimming quickly to the bank
In angry indignation,
He saw the woman waving
Which caused him more frustration.

'Put yourself through your mangle
With your washing load,
Iron your face and crimp it – then
You might look decent Toad.'

Toad didn't stop to answer;
His face was set and grim.
He wanted tangible revenge:
It stood in front of him!

He overtook the barge horse,
Untied the rope which towed;
Then jumping on the horse's back
Away he quickly rode.

Happily Toad made his way
Along a winding lane;
Once when he turned he faintly heard
The woman call in vain.

'Bring back my horse,' he heard her cry.
'Or you'll hear from the law.'
Toad laughed and chuckled to himself,
'I've heard that one before.'

Toad rode the horse down byways
Enjoying the sun's warm feel,
But then his stomach rumbled –
He was ready for a meal.

Presently, feeling drowsy,
He gently stopped the horse
On a piece of common land
Adorned with yellow gorse.

He looked around and noticed
A gypsy caravan,
And sitting on a bucket was
A weather-beaten man.

A little fire was crackling,
A pot was on the fire,
And smells burst forth awaking
Toad's taste buds with desire.

He looked the gypsy up and down
And sniffed the pleasant smell;
The gypsy sat and smoked his pipe
And stared at him as well.

At length the gypsy said as one
Who lives his life outdoors,
'Tell me, do you want to sell
That mangy horse of yours?'

Toad was very startled and
Forgot his empty feeling;
He hadn't know that gypsies
Went in for barge-horse dealing.

He'd forgotten for a moment
That caravans need drawing,
Because his mind was taken up
With his stomach's gnawing.

It just had not occurred to him –
Indeed it seemed quite funny –
But now he thought he saw a way
To get both food and money.

'What!' he cried out to the man
In a self-righteous whine.
'Me, sell this strong and lovely steed,
This strapping horse of mine?

'Who's going to take the washing
To the clientele?' says he.
'Besides I'm far too fond of him
And he just dotes on me.'

'Love a donkey,' said the man.
Toad said simply, 'Never!
You see this fine young horse of mine
Is from good stock and clever.

'He's partly pedigree but not
The part you see of course;
He's also part prize Hackney –
A quite outstanding horse.

'No, it cannot be thought of,
Without him I would pine.
All the same, what would you give
For this fine horse of mine?'

The gypsy gave the horse a glance –
Sighed in a careless way,
'Shilling a leg and that's too much.'
And then he turned away.

'A shilling a leg,' cried hungry Toad;
The words came in a shout.
'Wait while I take a moment
To quickly work that out.'

Toad did sums on his fingers.
At last he called out 'Four!
Why that comes to just four shillings
And not a penny more!

'Oh no!' cried Toad with feeling.
'The daftest thing I've heard.'
'Make it five,' the gypsy said,
'And that's my final word.'

Toad pondered very deeply;
He thought it through and through.
Finally he said, 'Look here,
I'll tell you what we'll do.

'You let me have six shillings,
Cash on the nail of course,
And then as much as I can eat –
And you can have the horse.

'Now if that isn't good enough,
Well, I'll be on my way;
I know a man who's wanted him
For many a long day.'

The man gave Toad six shillings,
Then with no further talk
He went inside the cart and fetched
A cup, plate, knife and fork.

The gypsy pointed to the pot;
Toad loaded up his plate.
He ate the stew up hungrily –
It really was first rate.

When Toad had eaten all he could
Push down his throat by force,
He bade the gypsy a good day
And farewell to the horse.

The gypsy knew the river
And told him where to go,
So Toad set off now feeling
A warm and happy glow.

The sun was shining brightly,
He was nearing journey's end,
Eager now to be back home
And spend time with a friend.

He thought of his adventures,
How he came out the best.
'I'm such a clever Toad,' he cried
Pushing out his chest.

'There surely is no creature
Can equal my finesse,
Who beats off all his enemies –
Escapes from every mess.

'I broke out of that prison,
Escaped though they gave chase;
I snapped my fingers at them,
They vanished in a trace.

'I'm thrown into deep water by
A woman mean and fat;
I swim ashore and steal her horse,
And ride off just like that.

'I sell the horse for money,
And food – all I can load;
Oh yes, I am the handsome
Dashing, daring Mr Toad.'

He puffed up with conceit and then,
Composed a little song
All about himself – he sang
As he strode along.

He sang out loudly as he walked,
A truly happy Toad,
And after covering many miles
He reached the main high road.

And then he saw a distant speck
And it was growing near,
And then, a most familiar sound
Fell sweetly on his ear.

'This is something like,' said Toad,
'This is life for real.
I'll stop them and address them as
My brothers of the wheel.

'I'll pitch to them a little yarn.
The kind I've told before,
And then I'll cadge a lift, and then
I'll talk to them some more.

'And maybe with a bit of luck
They'll let me have a drive,
And I'll be brilliant Toad again,
Audacious and alive.

'And then I'll drive the motor car
Directly to Toad Hall.'
With that he stepped into the road
And gave a cheery call.

The car slowed to an easy pace
As it approached the Toad,
But when Toad saw the driver,
He sank onto the road.

It was the car he'd stolen
From the hotel yard.
Toad could not believe his eyes,
This really was so hard.

And the people were the same
As on that fateful day;
The same he'd watched at luncheon,
All talkative and gay.

He sank down in a shabby heap –
It really wasn't fair!
Poor Toad just murmured to himself
In desperate despair.

'Chains, police and prison.'
He cried aloud in vain,
'Oh fool! You'll now be living
On prison fare again.

'What did I go a-strutting for
In that silly way,
Stopping people on the road
Right in the light of day?

'I should have left at nightfall.
Slipped home quietly.
Oh stupid, silly, hopeless Toad!
What will become of me?'

The splendid motor car drew near –
Toad shook from limb to limb.
And then the car pulled over,
A few feet short of him.

Two well-dressed gentlemen stepped out,
And viewed the trembling heap.
'Oh dear, this is so very sad;
It makes you want to weep.

'Here's a frightened, poor, old thing,
A washer, I would say,
Clearly overcome by heat,
She's fainted quite away.

'We'll take her to the village
Which isn't very far.'
So tenderly they lifted Toad
Into the motor car.

Toad's heart, which had been beating fast,
Soon ceased to pound and race
When he began to hear them talk
And saw a friendly face.

His courage was returning;
He felt better now he knew
That he remained unrecognised –
Once more his boldness grew.

So cautiously Toad opened
First one – then both – his eyes;
'Look I think she's coming round,'
A man said with surprise.

'She's starting to look better.
Improving, I'll be bound.
Our attention and fresh air
Are helping bring her round.

'How are you feeling, ma'am?' he asked.
The Toad began to stir.
'Oh I feel so much better now –
Thank you kindly, sir.'

'That's right,' the man continued.
'You've been a little ill.
Don't try to talk too much just yet;
Lie there and keep quite still.'

'I'll do as you suggest,' said Toad,
'But could I change my place
And sit in front where I can feel
The air full on my face?'

'A good idea,' exclaimed the man,
'Air's a great reviver.'
So carefully they moved the Toad
To sit beside the driver.

And now Toad felt himself again,
His heart began to pound;
He felt the same old feelings –
Sat up and looked around.

And quickly they possessed him,
They made him feel alive.
'It's fate,' he chuckled to himself,
'For I was born to drive.'

'Please sir,' he said, 'I wonder,'
With all his usual guile,
'Might I take the steering wheel,
Just for a little while.

'I've been watching carefully.
I could drive this car;
I'd like to say I've driven,
Albeit not that far.'

The driver laughed out loudly,
Looked down and said, 'Oh my!'
But then one of the gentry said,
'Do let her have a try.

'I admire your spirit, ma'am.
I'm sure that you can manage.
Driver, let her have a go –
She won't do any damage.'

Toad leapt at once into the seat;
It was so good to feel
The throbbing of the engine and
To grip the steering wheel.

He listened to instructions
As if he had no notion
Of how a car was driven and
Then set the car in motion.

The gentlemen clapped loudly
And said it was sublime
To see a woman driving
So expertly – first time.

Toad built up the speed until
The men cried out with dread,
'Be careful, washerwoman .'
Toad laughed and lost his head.

The driver tried to stop him.
Toad pinned him to his seat;
He wouldn't let him ruin
This unexpected treat.

The rush of air upon his face,
The engine's roar again
And the power of the car
Befuddled Toad's weak brain.

'I'm not a washerwoman.
I'm famous Mr Toad,
The snatcher of fine motor cars,
King of the open road.

'Be quiet and sit still awhile,
So that you don't miss
Just what it's like to drive with Toad –
You'll find my driving bliss.'

'Seize him, seize him!' they all cried.
They grabbed in desperation.
'Seize the Toad and drag him off
To the next police station.'

They should have been more sensible,
They really should have thought
To stop the fast careering car
Before that sort of sport.

With a half turn of the wheel
Toad drove right through a hedge.
The car plunged deeply into mud
At a horse-pond's edge.

Toad went flying through the air
Just like a graceful swallow;
It was fun but then he thought,
'I wonder if they'll follow?'

He landed in the soft green grass
With a forceful thump,
And then he saw the car was smashed,
It lay a useless lump.

The gentlemen and driver,
As far as he could see,
Encumbered by their heavy coats
Were floundering helplessly.

He struggled up and off he ran,
As fast as he could go;
He huffed and puffed and panted till
His pace began to slow.

Relaxing then into a walk,
He laughed from sheer elation.
'Old Toad again!' he cried aloud
In vain self-admiration.

'Who was it got himself a lift?
No-one else would dare.
Who got moved into the front
Just to get some air?

'And who was it, who drove the car
To its limit and beyond?
Who taunted them and called them names,
Then tipped them in a pond?

'Who got away by flying
Through the air? Why me!
Who left his foes stuck in the mud
Where they deserved to be?'

He carried on in this smug way –
His normal boastful air –
Until a noise from far behind
Turned pleasure to despair.

He saw the police were coming.
'Oh horror, oh dear, no!'
They were running after him
As fast as they could go.

'Oh what a stupid ass I am.
I've had it now for sure.'
He gasped out loud and sprinted;
Now on the run once more.

'I'm such a frightful fool,' he cried,
'And so absurdly vain;
I promise I will never go
A-swaggering again.'

His legs were getting very tired;
He took a look around
And to his utter horror,
Saw they were gaining ground.

And he could hear them closing in,
Now they were right behind:
He plunged on, running wildly
As though completely blind.

He turned his head to look again
At his triumphant foe –
But then the earth sank under him
And Toad cried out, 'Oh no!'

He found that he was falling.
He grasped out at thin air;
Then splash! He hit some water
And gurgled in despair.

He'd fallen in a river
Which was both deep and wide;
He surfaced and then tried to grab
The reeds along its side.

He simply could not get a grip
And gasped out as he swam;
'Oh my, oh my, it serves me right!
Oh what a fool I am!'

But then he saw a big, dark hole
And stretching with his paw,
He grabbed the edge to save himself
From sinking down once more.

He hung on tight and bit by bit,
He slowly pulled his chin
Above the edge – he gasped and stared
At something bright within.

It moved towards him slowly,
A face began to grow.
It looked just like a kindly face
He had some cause to know.

Brown and small, with whiskers
As neat as any cat;
Soft and sleek and silky –
It was his friend the Rat.

A band of well-armed weasels

SUMMER TEARS

Rat gripped the Toad's neck firmly
And pulled him through the hole;
Toad stood there wet and soaking,
A poor, bedraggled soul.

But his damp spirits soon revived
Now he was with a friend;
He thought that his adventures
At last, were at an end.

He could relinquish his disguise
And put it in the past.
'Oh Rat,' he cried, 'It's really great
To see a friend at last.

'You've no idea just where I've been,
Travelling many a mile;
Such wild escapes, such dangers –
I know they'll make you smile.

'Been in a horrid prison,
Got out of it of course;
Thrown in a smelly, foul canal
But stole a bargee's horse.

'Sold him for loads of money –
That was really fun –
Hunted and chased all over,
Out there and on the run.

'I've been in some tight places,
The trials that I've been through –
You won't believe the half of it
When I tell it to you.'

'Stop that!' the Rat said gravely,
'I've never heard such tosh.
Take yourself upstairs at once
And go and have a wash.

'Get out of all those silly rags,
You're like a washer-wife;
I've never seen a shabbier thing,
Never in my life.

'You can wear some clothes of mine,
I'm sure they'll fit you too.
Stop swaggering and boasting;
I've had enough of you.'

Toad thought about not going –
He didn't move, just sat;
He didn't want more orders,
Especially from Rat.

But catching his reflection in
The mirror on the wall –
The image didn't make him look
A cultured Toad at all.

When Toad came back in clean, dry clothes
Silence reigned a while;
Then Rat said with some sympathy
And a reassuring smile…

'I do not want to add more pain
To all you've so far had,
But don't you think you've really been
An awfully silly lad?

'You readily admit there were
Some foul things done to you:
You've been thrown into deep water,
And by a woman too.

'I cannot understand you, Toad;
Where is the fun in that?
It really quite defeats me,' said
The stern, yet kindly Rat.

But he had even more to say;
There was much more to come.
'Cars have brought you only grief
Since you set eyes on one.

'If you're involved with motor cars
As generally you are,
In heaven's name why must you steal
Someone else's car?

'Spend your money if you want,
Crash cars if it's great fun,
But theft has turned you into
A convict on the run.

'Do you think I like to hear,
As I have lately heard,
That I'm the chap who's friendly with
A notorious jailbird?

'When will you start behaving?
When will this nonsense end?
And when can we be proud once more
To know you as a friend?'

Now Toad could on occasions see
Another's point of view,
Even when determined
To see a project through.

For though while Rat was talking
Toad sighed, 'But it was fun,'
By the time the Rat had finished
It seemed their minds were one.

'You're right,' the Toad agreed at last.
'How right you always are.
I swear I never want to see
Another flashy car.

'I hate them since that ducking.
My paws are red and raw.
I promise that I'll now behave,
Act properly once more.

'Fact is while I was choking
With water in my throat,
I had a really great idea
About a motor boat.

'But don't take on like that, dear Rat,
Please, let's not have a row.
It was only just a thought;
We'll leave it there for now.

'We'll have some piping coffee
And eat a tasty snack,
Then I'll stroll down to dear Toad Hall,
I'm eager to get back.

'I've had enough adventures –
Enough of silly crimes.
I want to get things going,
Enjoy some quiet times.'

'Take a stroll down to Toad Hall!'
Came Rat's loud, piercing shout.
'Whatever are you thinking of,
What are you on about?

'Toad, don't you know what's happened?
You mean you haven't heard?'
'What's that?' the Toad asked nervously.
'I haven't heard a word.'

'You mean to tell me,' yelled the Rat,
'You haven't heard at all,
How all the stoats and weasels
Have occupied Toad Hall?'

'What! Wild Wooders?' Toad cried out,
He shook from head to toe.
He leant across the table and
His tears began to flow.

'Go on,' he whimpered. 'Tell me, Rat,
Tell me the worst of it.
I'll pull myself together.
Tell every little bit.'

'When you got into trouble
Through your reckless spree,
When you, how can I put it, Toad,
Gave up society.

'Well, it was talked about a lot,
Everywhere round here.
Some fellow creatures sympathised;
Others did not, I fear.

'And animals took different sides,
As you'd have guessed they would:
Not just on the riverside
But over in the Wood.

'All the river-bankers –
They backed you in the main,
But the Wild Wood crowd all said,
"We won't see Toad again."

'Mole and Badger stuck it out
And said they were quite wrong;
That's the sort of friends they are –
Stood by you all along.

'They argued it from history;
They said there were no laws
That ever had been known to work
Against such cheek as yours.

'They said that with your money
You'd soon be free as air,
So they moved to your mansion,
Arranged to settle there…

'To keep it aired and ready for
Your prayed for quick return.
But this is now the painful bit
Which sadly you must learn.

'For one dark night those faithful friends
Sat by a fire of logs;
It was blowing hard outside
And raining cats and dogs.

'A band of well-armed weasels
Crept quietly up the drive,
And through the kitchen garden
Ferrets started to arrive.

'Meanwhile a company of stoats
Had quietly occupied
All the rear rooms at Toad Hall
And some along the side.

'Deep in conversation,
Mole and Badger heard no sound,
Until the villains entered,
They came from all around.

'They fought as best they could,
Though taken by surprise,
But one can't beat off hundreds
However hard one tries.

'They beat the pair up thoroughly.
They told them both to "Get!"
They threw your two most faithful friends
Into the cold and wet.'

Here the Toad turned out to be
A most unfeeling figure:
A smile broke out across his face
And he began to snigger.

Just as quickly he assumed
A solemn face, however,
Disguising his amusement
With extreme endeavour.

'Then they moved into Toad Hall.
They're living there still now,
Lying round in bed all day,
Going on anyhow.

'They've eaten every scrap of food,
Recounting silly jokes
About the police and prison,
And telling all the folks…

'That they have come to stay for good.'
Toad looked across at Rat,
'Have they indeed!' His anger boiled,
'Well I'll not stand for that.'

'You had better calm yourself;
It's really hopeless, Toad.'
But Toad was off and marching
Head bent, along the road.

As he approached his former home
He broke into a run,
Only stopping when he saw
A ferret with a gun.

'Who goes there?' the ferret shrieked.
'Stuff and nonsense!' Toad replied,
'Get out of there this minute.'
But then his bluster died.

The ferret simply aimed his gun
Without a further word.
Scared Toad dropped flat upon the road;
A bang was all he heard.

Scrambling to his feet he ran
As though he'd sprouted wings,
And as he ran he heard them laugh
And shout out horrid things.

'What did I tell you?' Rat exclaimed.
'I won't give up,' Toad cried.
He took Rat's boat and rowed towards
The mansion's river side.

When he arrived in sight of home
He rested on his oars;
Everything seemed quiet in
The house and out of doors.

In fact the house seemed empty
From what he could discern,
Apparently just waiting
For roaming Toad's return.

He rowed along a little creek
When something fell and crashed;
A rock had dropped from high above
And now the boat was smashed.

It filled with water and then sank.
Toad struggled to get free,
Then looking up he saw two stoats
Sitting in a tree.

Indignant Toad at once struck out
For the nearest shore.
The stoats just sat there laughing
Until their sides were sore.

They laughed until they nearly fell,
They laughed till they were hoarse;
The creatures nearly had two fits –
That's one fit each of course!

Toad retraced his weary steps
To faithful Rat once more;
'What did I tell you, Toad?' said Rat.
'It's as I said before.

'Now you've lost my lovely boat,
Ruined a suit of clothes –
How you ever keep your friends
Heaven only knows.'

Toad admitted that he'd paid
A price for what he'd seen;
He said he knew how silly
And foolish he had been.

He said, 'From now on I will be
Both sensible and nice,
And I will take no action
Without your sound advice.'

'If that is really so,' said Rat
In his good natured chatter,
'We'll talk to Mole and Badger
About this vexing matter.'

'Oh yes, of course,' said thankful Toad,
'The Badger and the Mole.
Where are those two fine fellows?
Tell me about their role.'

'They've both camped out,' said solemn Rat,
'In cold and rain and all,
In order to keep watch upon
Your lovely home, Toad Hall.

'Living very rough by day,
And lying hard by night,
Making plans and scheming
On how to put things right.

'You don't deserve such friends, you know –
Of that I am quite sure.
Some day you will be sorry
Not to respect them more.'

'I'm a rotten beast,' sobbed Toad.
'Oh Rat, I know you're right.
I will go and look for them,
Out in the cold, dark night.

'I'll share their hardships with them,
But Ratty – well I say –
Did I hear the merry chink
Of dishes on their way?

'I'm really famished, that I am.
Oh, what a welcome sight.'
And Toad jumped up excitedly
Croaking with delight.

'Come on, Ratty, let's tuck in.
Oh this is great – hooray!'
Rat knew Toad hadn't eaten
Since earlier that day.

And so they sat themselves right down –
Rat told the Toad to eat,
And when they'd finished dining
Each took a comfy seat.

Then they heard a hammering
Upon the outside door;
Toad's thoughts turned very quickly to
The long arm of the law.

Rat jumped onto his feet at once
To see who'd come to call;
He came back with the Badger;
They entered from the hall.

Badger looked quite troubled,
His shoes all streaked in grime,
But then he never looked that smart,
No, not at any time.

He wandered slowly up to Toad
And shook him by the paw.
'Welcome home,' the Badger said.
'It's hard for you, I'm sure.

'This is a poor homecoming, Toad.'
He turned his soulful eye
Upon the supper Rat had laid
And took a slice of pie.

Toad was worried by these words
And he began to fret;
Rat whispered quietly to Toad,
'Don't speak to him just yet.

'You know how he gets tetchy
When ready for his food;
Give it half an hour or so,
And he will change his mood.'

But as they waited patiently
A knock came at the door.
Rat hurried off to open it
Just as he'd done before.

He came back with the caller –
This time it was the Mole –
And he looked weary and worn out,
A dismal looking soul.

'Hooray! Here's Toad,' the Mole cried out
As he came through the door;
'I can't believe you're home again,
Safe and sound once more.

'Why Toad you are so clever!
How did you get free?'
Rat tried to stop excited Mole –
For he could clearly see…

That Toad was puffing up with pride.
'Clever? Not me,' he said.
'I merely strove to put to use
The brain that's in my head.

'According to one valued friend
I've not achieved that much,
But many would insist that I
Possess a magic touch.

'Who was it broke from prison,
Escaping from the law?
Hijacked a railway engine
Just with a single paw.

'Disguised himself and got away
From every dangerous jam:
Clever? Oh, no not me, dear Mole –
A stupid ass I am.

'Listen here and you can judge
If what I did was fickle.'
'Talk while I eat,' said hungry Mole
Grabbing cheese and pickle.

Toad showed off his bag of cash.
'Look, Mole,' he cried with feeling.
'I earned this pile of money through
Some clever barge-horse dealing.'

'Toad, be quiet,' said the Rat,
Showing his frustration.
'Tell us very quickly, Mole,
What's the situation?'

'The situation is about
As hopeless as can be;
What's to be done,' replied the Mole,
'Completely baffles me.

'Badger and I explore the scene
And each time it's the same.
They point their guns towards us
And shout a horrid name.'

'What Toad should do,' proclaimed the Rat,
As if he really knew…
'No he shouldn't,' shouted Mole.
'I know what Toad should do…'

'Well, I shan't do it anyway,'
Toad said and stamped the ground.
'I've had as much as I can take
Of being bossed around.

'Just remember it's my house
That you all talk about…'
And at this point their tempers flared
And they began to shout.

The noise became quite deafening,
Till a deep voice was heard:
'Be quiet, all of you, at once!'
Nobody spoke or stirred.

The Badger having said these words
Turned back to eat some cheese,
And so immense was their respect
For his great qualities…

That not another word was said
Till he'd finished his repast.
Then standing up and looking round
The Badger spoke at last.

'Now Toad,' he said severely,
'You tiresome little sham,
Aren't you ashamed of what you've done?
I'm sure I know I am.

'What would your well-loved father say
If he could see this sight?
What would my dear old friend have thought
If he'd been here tonight?

'Do you believe your goings on
Would strike him as good fun?
He would have been ashamed of you,
His heir and only son.'

Toad began to shake with sobs,
Soft tears rolled down his face.
'There, there,' said Badger kindly,
'We won't dwell on your disgrace.

'Never mind now – dry your eyes.'
Toad grudgingly uncurled.
'But Mole is right regarding stoats –
The best guards in the world.

'They're far too strong for us I fear;
We can't attack the place.'
'Then it's all over,' sobbed the Toad,
And once more hid his face.

The Badger was upset to see
Poor Toad in such bad form.
'Now there are other ways,' he said,
'Than taking it by storm.

'Cheer up Toad – I've more to say
Which will surprise you so,
For now I'm going to tell you of
A secret you don't know.'

Toad sat up and looked around
And slowly ceased to weep.
He loved a secret for it was
A thing he couldn't keep.

'There is a secret passageway,'
Said Badger solemnly,
'That leads right from the river side
Up to Toad Hall, you see.'

'Oh nonsense, Badger,' Toad replied.
'They're silly yarns, I fear;
They're spun in public houses
In villages round here.'

'My dear young friend,' said Badger
In tone severe and low,
'Your father was much worthier
Than others that I know.

'He was a valued friend of mine,
Both close and very true,
He told me quite a lot of things
He never told to you.

'That passage he discovered,
Repaired and cleared it out;
One day it would prove useful,
Of that he had no doubt.

'He showed it to me saying,
"Don't tell my son – he's young;
He's not a bad boy really
But he can't hold his tongue.

' "He has a silly manner,
Acts like a child of six;
Only tell him of it if
He's really in a fix." '

The others, anxious, looked at Toad
To see what he would say,
But he could be quite reasonable,
And took it the right way.

'I know I talk a lot,' he said,
'And earn myself much glory,
My friends come round, we have a drink,
I tell a witty story.

'And then I talk and I expand
Upon some new sensation –
You must remember that I have
The gift of conversation...'

'Now I've found out a thing or two,'
Said Badger, as before.
'Otter called and gave a knock
Upon the tradesman's door.

'You know old Otter,' Badger said,
'There's simply no-one bolder.
He dressed himself up as a sweep
With brushes on his shoulder.

'He asked to sweep the chimney and
He heard somebody say
That there's a feast tomorrow night
To mark a special day.

'It's the Chief Weasel's birthday,
It's in the dining hall;
They'll be eating and a-drinking,
And carrying on and all.

'And while they are all gathered there
Thinking they're so clever,
They'll be relaxed and careless
And have no arms whatever.'

'But they'll have guards around the place,'
Said Rat – his face looked black.
'I'm afraid you're dead right there,'
Came Badger's answer back.

'That's where the passageway comes in,'
Badger addressed his friends.
'We'll creep in through the pantry,
That's where the passage ends.

'Right next to the dining hall,
For there it won't be manned.'
'That squeaky board,' the Toad cried out,
'Oh, now I understand.'

'We'll creep out from the pantry,
From in that deep, dark hole,
And give them all a big surprise,'
Cried the excited Mole.

'And with our pistols and our swords,
And our sticks,' yelled Rat,
'And whack 'em really hard,' screamed Toad,
'And that will make them scat.'

'Very well,' said Badger
In his sound, solid way,
'Our plan is now quite settled;
There's nothing more to say.

'So as it's getting rather late
Let's get ourselves to bed.'
They tottered off and tired Toad
Had wild thoughts in his head.

He thought they'd keep him wide awake,
But soon he fell asleep
And dreamt of cells and prisons,
Deep in a castle keep.

Toad was so tired that he slept on
Quite late into the morn,
And by the time he tottered down,
With many a groan and yawn…

His friends had finished breakfast,
And Mole was out somewhere,
While Badger calmly read the news,
Relaxing in a chair.

But on the other hand the Rat
Was running round and round,
Accumulating weapons in
Four mounds upon the ground.

'Here's a sword for Toad and Mole
And one for Badger too.'
He went on till the modest piles
Just grew and grew and grew.

'That's very well,' said Badger
Viewing the busy Rat,
'But let's get past those silly stoats
And we won't need all that.

'I tell you it will only take
The four of us – no more;
With clubs and sticks in half a tick
We'll drive them out the door.

'I could do it on my own –
What's needed to be done –
I'm only taking you along
So you can have some fun.'

Rat polished his gun barrel
And quietly then sighed;
'It will be just as well,' he said,
'To err on safety's side.'

Toad picked up a hefty stick
And swung it round his head;
'I'll learn 'em to invade my house,'
He threateningly said.

'Don't say "learn 'em", Toad,' said Rat,
Checking a rifle's bore.
The Badger turned to Rat and asked,
'What are you nagging for?

'They're the same words what I use.
They've always got me through;
So if they're good enough for me,
They're good enough for you.'

Presently the Mole came in,
Flung off his overcoat,
'I've been having lots of fun
Conversing with a stoat.

'I got the thought this morning when
I saw that funny dress,
Worn by old Toad when he came back
Looking such a mess.

'I went to Toad Hall wearing it,
As boldly as you please;
The sentries with their pistols
Were sitting in the trees.

' "Good morning to you, gentlemen,"
Calm as you like, I say.
"Want any of your washing done,
Or ironing today?"

'They looked at me quite haughtily
And said, "Clear off, my beauty.
We don't discuss our washing needs
While we're on sentry duty."

' "Or at any time," says I.
Ho, ho – it was such fun.'
'Poor silly creature,' Toad replied,
'What have you gone and done?'

'The sergeant then in charge, he said,
"Good woman, run away.
Don't keep my men here talking
While they're at work today."

' "It's run away good woman!
Well, not for long," I say,
"It will not be the likes of me
Who'll have to run away."

'The stoats pricked up their little ears.
The sergeant bade me go.
He said, "Now don't you mind her lads.
Whatever could she know?

' "She's talking utter nonsense,
Of that you can be sure."
"Sergeant, is that so?" says I,
"Well let me tell you more.

' "My daughter works for Badger…"
That made them change their tune…
"So I know what I'm saying –
And you'll know pretty soon.

' "A hundred fearsome Badgers will
Attack this very night;
They'll come across the paddock and
You know how Badgers fight.

' "Then six boats filled with Rats with guns
And pistols swords and all,
Will come up river and land in
The gardens of Toad Hall.

' "And then the death-or-glory Toads
Will storm through like a flood,
Destroying all who cross their path,
And yelling "Death and blood."

'And then I quickly ran away
But crept back through a ditch;
They all looked very nervous,
Every one a-twitch.

'I heard the stoats all saying,
"Whatever's to be done?
Those weasels will be feasting
And having lots of fun…

' "While we are likely to be killed
By bullet or a knife;
They'll be singing songs while we
Are fighting for our life." '

'Oh you silly ass!' cried Toad,
'You've spoiled what we're to do.'
'Clever Mole,' the Badger said,
'I have great hopes for you.'

Toad was really jealous,
It's true to say, however,
He simply couldn't see at all
How Mole had been so clever.

But luckily before he had
A chance to show his mood,
The bell rang out for luncheon and
They went to have some food.

The Badger, after lunch, slipped off,
'For some sleep,' he said,
'Because it will be very late
Before we get to bed.'

The anxious and hard-working Rat
Resumed his task with care.
Mole drew his arm through Toad's and said,
'Let's go and get some air.'

He begged the Toad to tell him
The whole thing – to the end.
And with no-one to check him, Toad
Regaled his eager friend.

He told his tale in detail,
Left everything intact –
Except the way he told it was
More fictional than fact.

There'd be a speech, of course, by Toad

TOAD'S HOMECOMING

Rat called them to the parlour
As dusk began to fall,
So he could get them ready for
The battle of Toad Hall.

He was resolute and earnest,
It all took quite a while;
He made each one of them stand still
Beside their little pile.

He handed each a studded belt
Of leather, strong and broad,
And then into each belt he thrust
A sharp and trusty sword.

The Badger laughed and said, 'I won't
Need these to make them flee,
But if it pleases you, dear Rat,
It does no harm to me.

'I'm just going to use my stick
To do what I must do.'
The Rat replied, 'But Badger, please,
These will take care of you.

'I do not want to take the blame
If all goes badly wrong
Because some things were left behind
We should have had along.'

Badger took a lantern and
A stick which he held fast.
'Now, follow me,' he gruffly said:
'Mole first, Rat next, Toad last.

'And look here Toad – don't chatter
As you're prone to do.
For if you do I'll send you back,
And that I promise you.'

The Toad was really all fired up
To fight the opposition,
And so without another word
He took up his position.

Badger climbed into a hole
Down by the river's edge;
Mole and Rat both followed him
But Toad tripped on its ledge.

He fell into the water;
They grabbed him – rubbed him down.
Badger then said angrily,
And with a fearful frown…

'Pull yourself together, Toad,
Or next time you will find
I won't be quite so easy and
We'll just leave you behind.'

Then they reached the passage
Well hidden by the river;
It was cold and very damp
And Toad began to shiver.

He trembled from the dreadful thought
Of what they were to do,
And also from the fact that he
Was soaking wet right through.

Now Toad kept lagging at the rear;
The light was far ahead.
'Come on, Toad,' the Rat called out.
Scared Toad was filled with dread.

He thought that he'd get left behind,
So put on such a spurt
That they all bumped together
And landed in the dirt.

The Badger, very angry, then
Declared he was inclined
To stop the Toad from coming
And make him stay behind.

He nearly lost his temper as
The poor Toad sniffed and cried;
Rat pleaded with the Badger
Till he was pacified.

They crept along then as before,
Rat bringing up the rear,
Till Badger said, 'I think that now
We're getting very near.'

Suddenly from far away
They heard the faintest sound.
Toad's nervous fears then all returned –
His heart began to pound.

They heard a noise of cheering
And banging on a table.
'Steady,' Badger calmly said,
As only he was able.

The passageway sloped upwards;
The noise broke out once more:
'Hip, hip hooray!' they heard above,
Then stamping on the floor.

And shouting out and hooting,
Oh, what a row they made,
They clearly didn't think they had
A need to be afraid.

'They're having fun,' said Badger,
Then before them they all saw
The passageway had reached its end;
Above them a trapdoor.

Such a noise was going on
They knew they'd not be heard.
'We'll force the door,' the Badger said.
'Push when I give the word.'

They leant against the trapdoor,
It creaked and opened wide;
They climbed into the pantry and
Then stood there side by side.

The clamour coming from the room
Was loud as it could be,
Then a voice called 'Silence!' and
Addressed the company.

'I do not want to keep you, but
Let me propose a toast,
To good old Mr Toad who is
Our absent, generous host.'

Laughter broke out all around.
'Quiet – now please attend:
To good old Toad – to honest Toad –
To Toad, our absent friend.'

'Let me at him now,' snarled Toad.
'And I'll give him what for.'
'Hold a minute,' Badger said,
And lifted up a paw.

The voice continued speaking:
'Now I won't keep you long;
You see I've been composing –
I'd like to sing a song.

'I think you'll guess the subject.'
He was tapping out the beat,
'Toad he went a-pleasuring
All gaily down the street.'

The Badger gripped his heavy stick,
Turned to his friends and cried,
'The hour has come!' He grabbed the door
And flung it open wide.

What squealing and a-screeching
And squeaking filled the air
As all the weasels dived and fled
Or tried to hide somewhere.

Under tables, under chairs
And in the old fireplace,
Wherever weasels tried to hide
Our heroes gave them chase.

The mighty Badger's cudgel
Whistled through the air.
And it was pandemonium,
Creatures everywhere.

'A Mole, a Mole!' cried out the Mole.
He made this his war cry.
The Rat was fighting desperately,
Prepared to do or die.

Toad, frenzied with excitement,
And also injured pride,
Searched out the proud Chief Weasel,
Although he tried to hide.

' "Toad he went a-pleasuring…"
I'll show him,' he said.
And finding the Chief Weasel crashed
His cudgel on his head.

Although there were but four of them,
So fearsome was the fray,
The room seemed full of creatures,
Brown, yellow, black and grey.

And they were on the warpath
With chilling, fearful cries,
With swinging clubs and thrashing swords
And angry, blazing eyes.

The weasels all fled squealing
With terror and dismay;
They ran through open windows,
Up chimneys – any way.

The fighting was soon over,
They had achieved their ends,
And boldly they strode up and down,
These four triumphant friends.

Badger, breathing deeply,
Wiped his perspiring brow.
'Mole, do one small thing,' he said,
'Just cut along right now…

'And check on those stoat sentries;
See if they're still in sight,
Though I suspect we will not hear
Much more from them tonight.'

Then they laid up a table.
'Get me a knife and fork,
I want some grub,' said Badger in
His rough and ready talk.

'And Toad, get moving, stir your stumps
Get back onto your feet;
Least you can do is give your friends
A decent meal to eat.'

Toad felt annoyed and angry,
His face looked cross and grim,
He thought the Badger had been curt
And rather hard on him.

He wished that he'd say pleasant things,
The way he did to Mole,
Especially as he thought he'd proved
He was a fearless soul.

He'd walloped the Chief Weasel
As hard as he was able;
He'd sent that old Chief Weasel
Flying 'cross the table.

Then just as they sat down to eat
The busy Mole returned;
'It's over,' he reported,
'From what I've just discerned.

'When the stoats heard so much shrieking,
The yells and screams and all,
And such a frantic uproar
Coming from the Hall,

'They acted in a desperate way
As only cowards can;
Some stoats threw down their rifles,
Took to their heels and ran.

'The others held their ground awhile,
Said, "What's it all about?"
But then they thought they'd been betrayed
When weasels all rushed out.

'Stoats grappled with the weasels,
Who fought to get away,
They wrestled, punched and wriggled
In a frightful fray.

'They rolled and fell and ran and slipped,
Each frightened and a-quiver;
They rolled on one another till
They rolled into the river.

'They've all gone now,' the Mole declared,
'Run off into the night;
I've gathered up the rifles,
So everything's all right.'

'Excellent,' said Badger
His mouth full up with trifle,
'But there's just one more thing to do
Now you've got every rifle.

'I wouldn't trouble you again
But you're the only one
I know that I can really trust
To see a job's well done.

'So please take all these prisoners.'
He pointed to the floor,
'And make them clean some bedrooms –
Then chuck them out the door.

'Then sit down here and have some food –
It's really quite first rate.
Mole, I'm pleased with you,' he said,
Then turned back to his plate.

Later on the Mole returned
And said, 'The job is done;
I've kicked them off the property,
Each and every one.'

Toad tried to hide his envy
And keep it out of sight.
'Thank you so much dear Mole,' he said,
'For all your help tonight.'

The Badger was extremely pleased:
'Well spoken, Toad,' he said.
Then they all finished supper and
Exhausted, went to bed.

~ ~ ~

Next morning Toad came down the stairs
To breakfast very late:
All he could find was dry, burnt toast
And eggshells on a plate.

A coffee pot half empty
Put him into a mood.
'Fine thing,' he thought 'that even here
I can't get decent food.'

Mole and Rat were both outside
Taking the morning air;
Badger was busy reading,
Snug in a comfy chair.

It was his favourite pastime,
Just where he liked to be;
His glasses perched upon his nose
And sitting comfortably.

Toad made the best of breakfast,
Then sat with vacant stare,
Till Badger said, 'I think we four
Should mark this fine affair.

'We must arrange a banquet,
And make it special too;
We'll have a celebration –
It's the least that we can do.'

'All right,' Toad said to Badger,
'I'll do just as you say.
But why d'you want a banquet in
The middle of the day?'

'Don't be so stupid,' Badger said.
'You really are a dunce!
The banquet will be after dark –
But invites go at once.

'And you will have to write them out
So Toad, do what you're told;
You've headed paper with "Toad Hall"
Embossed in blue and gold.

'Go and write to all your friends –
And, Toad, I have a hunch
That you will get them finished by
The time we have our lunch.'

'What! Write out rotten letters?'
Selfish Toad was most dismayed.
'I want to go and tell my friends
About our daring raid.

'I want to tell them that I'm back,
They'll all want to know;
I haven't time to write out…
Wait a minute though.

'Why, of course, dear Badger.
What is my joy or fun
Compared with that of others?
I see it must be done.

'The banquet must be ordered;
Now Badger, you decide –
Then go and join our carefree friends
In the grounds outside.

'Just leave me to my cares and toil,
And please don't think of me;
I sacrifice this morning to
My special friends, you three.'

Badger looked suspiciously
At Toad's now pleasant mood,
But what could be the motive for
This altered attitude?

Badger shuffled from the room,
The door closed in his rear;
Toad hurried to the table,
He'd had a great idea.

He'd write out invitations
With details of the raid;
How he had led the fighting –
The impact he had made.

He'd hint at his adventures
And where they all had led;
There'd be a programme also;
He sketched it in his head.

There'd be a speech, of course, by Toad –
One of his very best –
Then an address and then a song,
And then he'd take a rest.

Then another fine address
On subjects to inspire,
Such as 'Our Prison System' or
'Life with an English Squire'.

The idea made him happy;
He worked and sang a tune.
He finished all the letters as
The mantel clock struck noon.

Just then a message came, there was
A weasel at the door,
Asking could he help the Toad?
Toad said he could for sure.

'Deliver these,' he ordered.
The weasel was most willing.
Toad told him when he'd done it
He might give him a shilling.

They had their lunch and then Toad said,
'My friends, I beg your pardon,
Please help yourself to what you want.'
Then went off to the garden.

He thought he'd write out speeches
So he'd know what to say,
And when the Rat caught up with him
He tried to get away.

He realised the game was up –
It was confirmed for sure –
When Badger grabbed his other arm
With his big, furry paw.

They went into the smoking room
And sat him in a chair;
And then they stood in front of him –
Toad had a wary air.

'Now look here, Toad,' Rat started,
'I'm sorry I must say
Although this is your banquet
You cannot have your way.

'We want you now to understand,
So do not get it wrong,
There will be no more speeches
And not a single song.

'And try at last to grasp the fact
Whatever else you do,
This time we are not arguing,
This time we're telling you.'

Toad saw that he was truly trapped,
His pleasant dreams a-shatter.
'Can't I sing one little song?'
He pleaded, 'One won't matter.'

Rat hated to deny him
But said, 'Not even one.
It's no good Toad – we know full well
What you call having fun.

'Your songs are simply vanity,
All boasting and conceit;
You stand up making speeches –
You're never in your seat.

'And they're all filled with praise of self
And gross exaggeration.'
'And gas,' put in the Badger
For further explanation.

'You know it's for your own good, Toad,
You just don't keep it brief.
The time has come, you really must
Turn over a new leaf.

'It had to come to this some time,
The truth is hard, I fear,
But treat it as a turning point
In your august career.'

Toad was silent for a time,
The quietest of creatures.
Strong emotions could be seen
Competing on his features.

'You've convinced me, my dear friends.'
His voice came wearily.
'It was a small thing that I asked,
But what will be will be.

'I wanted just to blossom –
Expand and talk once more.
To hear for one more blissful time
The crowd's tumultuous roar.

'But I know you are in the right
And I, alas, am wrong;
So there'll be no more speeches
And not a single song.

'And, my friends, I promise you
I'll give up being vain;
You'll never have occasion
To blush for me again.

'Oh dear, this is a harsh old world.'
His voice was filled with gloom.
Then as the tears began to flow
He staggered to his room.

'Badger,' said the kindly Rat,
'I feel a brute, do you?'
'I know, I know,' said Badger,
'But we must see this through.

'We cannot let him carry on
As someone they all mock;
He has to be respected,
Not be a laughing-stock.

'We can't have stoats and weasels
Jeering as they do…
And what a bit of luck we stopped
That weasel getting through.

'For he was in a hurry
And held there in his paw,
The biggest load of rubbish
A creature ever saw.

'He had Toad's invitations.
I looked at one or two:
They were an absolute disgrace,
A horror to look through.

'I tore the whole lot up and now
The Mole is working hard,
Writing out a nicely phrased
And modest invite card.'

~ ~ ~

Finally the banquet hour
Was drawing very near.
Toad retired up to his room
And wiped away a tear.

He sat alone and thoughtful,
His brow upon a paw;
He pondered for a moment,
Then thought a little more.

Gradually his manner grew
More positive and cheered;
His face lost its unhappy frown
As bit by bit, it cleared.

And then he took to giggling in
A silly kind of way;
He locked the door and swiftly drew
The curtains on the day.

Then he arranged the bedroom chairs
And, swelling visibly,
He bowed, he coughed and then began
To sing a song with glee.

And to a spellbound audience
That he so clearly saw,
He sang with great emotion
And in a mighty roar.

The song was all about himself,
Both arrogant and vain,
And when he'd done he sang it all
Out loudly once again.

At last he breathed in deeply,
Let out a heavy sigh,
Then plastered down his scanty hair
To make himself look spry.

Then he unlocked the bedroom door
And rearranged the chairs,
And sallied forth to greet his guests
Assembling downstairs.

The animals all cheered him as
He entered the great hall
And said, 'How very brave you are!'
Toad murmured, 'Not at all.'

Otter tried to take him round –
And pulled him from behind,
But Toad said, 'No, the Badger,
He was the mastermind.

'And Mole and Rat – they took the brunt.
To them I owe my thanks,
For I did very little,
I just served in the ranks.'

The animals were puzzled –
Toad found it all such fun;
He knew he was of interest
To each and every one.

Badger had arranged it all,
It was a great success;
There was much chaff and laughter
About Toad's cleverness.

But through it all, Toad didn't show
A single trace of pride,
He merely murmured pleasantries
To friends on either side.

He looked at Rat and Badger,
His face just didn't crack;
He saw them both – quite open mouthed,
Astounded, staring back.

Some of the younger creatures
Within that motley throng
Began to shout for Toad to speak
Or sing a little song.

But Toad just simply shook his head
And looked down at the floor,
To indicate that he'd not be
Performing anymore.

And then by earnest small talk
And other little signs
He now conveyed that dinner would
Be run on different lines.

And so in all these little ways
He very clearly showed
That he was much reformed and now,
A very altered Toad.

~ ~ ~

After the lavish banquet
Life went on as before;
Before the huge disturbance of
The stoat and weasel war.

Toad sent the jailer's daughter
A locket on a chain;
He also sent a present to
The driver of the train.

And under strong compulsion
From Badger, stern of course,
He sent the fat barge woman
Some money for her horse.

And sometimes in the summer
Our heroes would walk through
The Wild Wood, as it now was safe
For all of them to do.

They would be seen by weasels
As they all made their way,
And if the young were naughty
The weasels would then say...

'Look and see who's walking by –
It's famous Mr Toad,
And there goes gallant Mr Rat
A-striding down the road.

'And mind you pay attention now,
So you remember well,
For there's the fearsome Mr Mole
Of whom you have heard tell.'

But if their young stayed naughty
And would not do as told,
The weasels knew a certain way
To make them good as gold.

They would tell them, 'If you don't
Behave at once, right now,
The terrible grey Badger
Will get to you somehow.'

It always had a good effect
And gave the young a scare,
But Badger liked young children, so
It wasn't really fair.

Also by Richard Cuddington

SHAKESPEARE'S TRAGEDIES
IN EASY READING VERSE

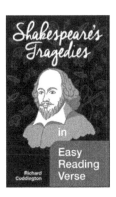

Richard Cuddington applies his Easy Reading Verse to Shakespeare's Tragedies. These are some of the Bard's most famous and compelling plays. Retold here in simple and engaging verse, the drama and excitement unfold with an urgency and momentum that captures the essence of the original plays.

Here the reader will meet Hamlet avenging his father's murder, Romeo risking all for his Juliet, Othello borne down with jealousy, Macbeth plotting to obtain Scotland's crown and many other colourful and doomed characters.

The sheer drama of some of Shakespeare's most memorable and highly acclaimed plays is captured here in fast moving, entertaining verse.

And when you know what each play is about you may well be encouraged to find out more about what makes these people tick by venturing into the original texts, having crept under the literary barrier and already found a way in by the back door.

SHAKESPEARE'S COMEDIES
IN EASY READING VERSE

Richard Cuddington offers his readers a new approach to
Shakespeare which acknowledges the Bard's stature as
England's finest poet and playwright but lays aside the
trappings of that greatness to reveal what made him
popular with his contemporary audiences and what can
still enchant us today – the stories.
Here in Easy Reading Verse the author retells the stories
of Shakespeare's Comedies with clarity, humour and a
modern directness. Readers will meet Shylock demanding
his pound of flesh, Jack Falstaff pursuing his 'merry
wives', Petruchio taming his Katherine and many other
unforgettable characters who leap off the page with the
immediacy of cartoon personalities.
The straightforward language with its bouncing, infectious
rhythms and uncomplicated verse add pace and humour
to each story as it rapidly unfolds. In this way the author
makes Shakespeare less intimidating to potential readers,
showing that England's greatest playwright can be fun and
encouraging all who enjoy these verses to sample the rich
pleasure of the original work.

SHAKESPEARE'S HISTORIES & ROMANCES IN EASY READING VERSE

Here in Richard Cuddington's Easy Reading Verse are
Shakespeare's Histories and Romances which take the
reader on two separate journeys. One through various
turbulent periods of English history – the other through
the slightly calmer waters of romance.
All the stories are told in clear and rhythmic verse which
enhances the many dramatic and romantic situations.
Readers will be entranced by the very diversity and
richness of the colourful plots.
Here we meet Richard the Second losing his throne,
Henry the Fifth conquering the French at Agincourt and
Richard the Third using all his dastardly wiles to keep the
crown. In contrast the Romances will introduce Prospero
whipping up a tempest, Pericles losing, then finding his
Thaisa and Palamon and Arcite fighting for the hand of
Emilia. A veritable pageant of drama, turmoil and intrigue
is encapsulated in these enthralling stories which are truly
some of the Bard's finest plays.
These adaptations are an enjoyable and riveting read and
act as an excellent bridge to the original texts.

SHAKESPEARE'S SONNETS
IN EASY READING VERSE

Richard Cuddington's light-hearted adaptation of Shakespeare's Sonnets captures the essence of the original texts but in a way that makes them instantly accessible and understandable to the modern reader.

Originally published in 1609, many critics believe the Sonnets come closer to revealing Shakespeare the man, than any of his other works. Written in the first person, the Sonnets expose an emotional range that has given them enduring appeal.

The author now applies his straightforward Easy Reading Verse to create a fresh interpretation of the Sonnets. Here in simple and enjoyable lyrics, the mysteries of the Sonnets are unravelled, and with the original texts also contained within the book, they act as an aid in the understanding of Shakespeare's masterpieces.

CHAUCER'S CANTERBURY TALES
IN EASY READING VERSE

For all its great reputation and the affection in which it is
held, Chaucer's Canterbury Tales, written in 14th century
Middle English, can actually be a daunting prospect to read.
Richard Cuddington now steps in with a novel approach
to Chaucer's famous gallery of pilgrims with their tales of
chivalry, romance, courtly love, treachery, avarice,
bawdiness, humour and nobility.
Whether you're new to the tales, or perhaps a teacher
looking to enthuse and stimulate your students, or simply
thinking of re-reading them, you will find here a
thoroughly entertaining and immediately accessible way in
to the storytelling genius of Chaucer in simple and
amusing rhyming verse.

CHARLES DICKENS' OLIVER TWIST IN EASY READING VERSE

Oliver Twist has been a family favourite ever since Charles Dickens gave birth to his marvellous story in 1837. It has been reproduced in many ways but now Richard Cuddington applies his Easy Reading Verse to recount this famous tale.

Here are all the familiar cast of characters – brought to life in fun, uplifting narrative verse that moves along at a vibrant pace. From the moment of Oliver's birth in the Workhouse, through all his adventures at the hands of Fagin and Bill Sikes until he finally finds a new life – there is never a dull moment.

The author has previously applied his straightforward, rhythmic style to The Complete Works of Shakespeare and Chaucer's Canterbury Tales and now turns to Dickens' famous story to retell it in a way that will have great appeal to children and adults alike.

CHARLES DICKENS' A CHRISTMAS CAROL
IN EASY READING VERSE

Charles Dickens' A Christmas Carol is arguably the most dearly loved Christmas story ever written – a favourite with the whole family. Whether you are one of the many fans of the story or possibly even new to the tale – you will surely enjoy this adaptation, written in fast moving, light-hearted verse. Author Richard Cuddington, who has already adapted the complete works of Shakespeare and Chaucer's Canterbury Tales into fun filled, narrative verse, now applies his rhythmic style to this famous classic. Here is Scrooge in all his miserly misery, slowly being converted from his former monstrous self into a being who really knows how to celebrate Christmas. The charming verse takes us on an unstoppable journey where we meet the Spirits of Christmas Past, Present and Future, the joyful Mr. Fezziwig and of course, the tragic but lovable figure of Tiny Tim. And on the way Scrooge dominates a tale that celebrates the joy of Christmas, encouraging a belief that we should embrace its spirit throughout the year.

Lightning Source UK Ltd.
Milton Keynes UK
UKOW06f2342290816

281771UK00014B/302/P